"In court," Brannhard said, "we'll have to show that the veridicator would have red-lighted if any of the Fuzzies had tried to lie."

"We need Fuzzy test witnesses to lie under veridication," Coombes added. "If they don't know how to lie, we'll have to teach a few. Do any of you gentlemen collect paradoxes? This one's a gem: To prove that Fuzzies tell the truth, we must first prove that they tell lies."

Everybody laughed, except Jack Holloway. He sat staring glumly at the table-top.

"So now, along with everything else, we've got to make liars out of them, too," he said. "I wonder what we'll finally end making them."

FUZZIES
AND OTHER PEOPLE
H. BEAM PIPER

ACE SCIENCE FICTION BOOKS
NEW YORK

FUZZIES AND OTHER PEOPLE

An Ace Science Fiction Book

PRINTING HISTORY
Ace Science Fiction edition / August 1984
Fourth printing / November 1986

ISBN: 0-441-26177-9

Ace Science Fiction Books are published by
The Berkley Publishing Group,
200 Madison Avenue, New York, New York 10016.
PRINTED IN THE UNITED STATES OF AMERICA

i.

Officially, on all the half-thousand human-populated planets of the Terran Federation, the date was September 14, 654 Atomic Era, but on Zarathustra it was First Day, Year Zero, Anno Fuzzy.

It wasn't the day that the Fuzzies were discovered—that had been in early June, when old Jack Holloway had found a small and unfamiliar being crouching in his shower stall at his camp up Cold Creek Valley on Beta Continent. He had made friends with the uninvited visitor and named him Little Fuzzy. A week later, four more Fuzzies and a baby Fuzzy had moved in, and Bennett Rainsford, then a field naturalist for the Institute of Xeno-Sciences, had seen them. They were completely new to him, too. He named the order Hollowayans, in honor of their discoverer, and called the genus Fuzzy and the species Holloway's Fuzzy: *Fuzzy fuzzy holloway*.

Fuzzies were erect bipeds, two feet tall and weighing fifteen to twenty pounds; their bodies were covered with silky golden fur. They had five-fingered hands with opposable thumbs, large eyes set close enough together for stereoscopic vision, and vaguely humanoid features. They seemed to know nothing of fire and, as far as Holloway and Rainsford were able to determine, they were incapable of speech. The fact that they spoke in the ultrasonic range was yet to be discovered. They made a few artifacts, however, and their reasoning ability amazed both men. As soon as he saw them, Rainsford insisted that Jack tape an account of them.

Twenty-four hours later, a number of people had heard that tape. One was Victor Grego, manager-in-chief of the Chartered Zarathustra Company. If, as seemed probable, these Fuzzies were sapient beings, Zarathustra automatically became a Class-IV inhabited planet. The Company's charter, conferring outright ownership of Zarathustra as a Class-III uninhabited planet, would be just as automatically void.

Grego's instinct was to fight, and he was a resourceful, resolute and ruthless fighter. He was not stupid, but some of his subordinates were; a week later, everybody on the planet had heard of the Fuzzies because a CZC executive named Leonard Kellogg was facing trial for murder—defined as the unjustified killing of any sapient being of any race whatsoever—for having kicked to death a Fuzzy named Goldilocks. Jack Holloway was similarly charged for having shot a Company gunman who had tried to interfere while he was administering a beating to Kellogg. Both cases, scheduled to be tried as one, would hinge on whether Fuzzies were sapient beings or just cute little animals. On the docket, it was *People of the Colony of Zarathustra* versus *Kellogg and Holloway,* but, beginning with Holloway's lawyer, Gus Brannhard, everybody was calling it *Friends of Little Fuzzy* versus *The Chartered Zarathustra Company.*

Little Fuzzy and his friends won, and when, on September 14, Chief Justice Frederic Pendarvis rapped with his gavel after reading what would go down in Federation legal history as the Pendarvis Decisions, Zarathustra became a Class-IV inhabited planet. The Space Navy had to take over until a new Colonial Government could be set up, and Bennett Rainsford was appointed Governor-General. The Zarathustra Company's charter was as dead as the Code of Hammurabi.

And *Fuzzy fuzzy holloway* was now *Fuzzy sapiens zarathustra.*

ii.

He didn't know that anybody called him a Fuzzy. When he and his kind called themselves anything, it was Gashta, "People."

There were animals, of course, but they weren't People. They couldn't talk, and they wouldn't make friends. Some were large and dangerous, like the three-horned *hesh-nazza,* or the night-hunting "screamers," or, worst of all, the *gotza* that soared on wide wings and swooped upon their prey. And some were small and good to eat, and the best of them were the *zatku* that scuttled on many legs among the grass and had to be broken out of their hard shells to get at the sweet white meat. One hunted and killed to eat, and one avoided being killed and eaten, and one tried to have all the fun one could.

Hunting was fun if game was not too scarce and one was not too hungry. And it was fun to outwit something that was hunting one and make a good escape. And it was fun to romp and chase one another through the woods, and to find new things; and it was fun to make a good sleeping-place and huddle together and talk until sleep came. And then, when the sun came back from its sleeping-place, it would be another day, and new and interesting things would happen.

It had always been like that, for as long as he could

remember, and that had been a long time. He couldn't
count how often the leaves had turned yellow and red
and then brown, and fallen from the trees. All those
who had been with the band when he was small were
gone, killed, or drifted away. Others had joined the
band, and now they called him Toshi-Sosso—Wise One,
One Who Knows Best—and they all did as he advised.
They had begun doing that when Old One had "made
dead." Old One had been a female; Little She, who
walked beside him now, was her daughter, one of the
very few Gashta who had been born alive and lived
more than very briefly.

It was Little She who saw the redberry bush even
before he did, and cried out in surprise:

"Look, redberries! Not finish yet; good to eat!"

It was late to find redberries; mostly they were brown
and hard now, and not good. There would be no more
for a long time, until after new-leaf time and bird-
nesting time. In the meantime, though, there would be
other good-to-eat things; soon, on a tree they all knew,
would be big brown nuts, and when the shells were
cracked they would be soft and good inside. He looked
forward to eating them, but he wondered why all the
good-to-eat things couldn't be at the same time. It
would be nice if they could, but that was how things had
always been.

They crowded around the bush, careful to avoid the
sharp thorns, picking berries and popping them into
their mouths and spitting out the seeds, laughing and
talking about how good they were and how nice it was
to find them so late. Some of the younger ones forgot,
in their excitement, to keep watch. He rebuked them:

"Keep watch, all time; look around, listen. You not
watch, something come, eat you."

Really, there was no danger. None of the animals they
had cause to fear were about, and none of them could
hear the voices of People. Still, one must never forget to
watch. Not remembering was how one made dead.

It wasn't fun, being Wise One. The others expected him to do all the thinking for them. That was not good. Suppose he made dead some time; who would think for them then? After they had eaten all the berries, they stood waiting for him to tell them what to do next.

"What we do now?" he asked them. "Where go?"

They all looked at him, wondering. Finally Other She, who had joined the band between bird-nesting time and groundberry time, before last leaf-turning time, said:

"Hunt for zatku. Maybe find zatku for everybody."

She meant, a whole zatku for each of them. They wouldn't; there weren't that many zatku. The day before yesterday, they had found two, only a few bites apiece. Besides, they would find none here among the rocks. Now was egg-laying time for zatku; they would all be where the ground was soft, to dig holes to lay their eggs. But they might find *hatta-zosa* here. He had seen young trees with the bark gnawed off. Hatta-zosa were good to eat, and if they killed two or three of them, it would be meat enough that nobody would be hungry.

Besides, killing hatta-zosa was fun. They were nearly as big as People, with strong jaws and sharp teeth, and when cornered they fought savagely. It was hard to kill them, and doing hard things was fun. He suggested hunting hatta-zosa, and they all agreed at once.

"Hatta-zosa stay among rocks." That was the young male they called Fruitfinder. "Rocks more at top of hill."

"Find moving-water," Big She offered. "Follow to where it come out of ground."

"Look for where hatta-zosa chew bark off trees."

That was Lame One. He was not really lame, but he had once hurt his leg and limped for a while, and after that they all called him Lame One because nobody could think of anything else to call him.

They started, line-abreast, each keeping sight of those on either side. They hunted as they went, not very

seriously, for they had just eaten the berries and if they
found hatta-zosa there would be much meat for everybody. Once, Wise One stopped at a rotting log and dug
in it with the pointed end of his killing-club, and found
a toothsome white grub. Once or twice he heard somebody chasing one of the little yellow lizards. Finally they
came to a small stream and stopped, taking turns drinking and watching. They they followed it up to the spring
where it came out of the ground.

This would be a good place to come back to if
anything chased them. Trees grew close to it, with sharp
branches; a gotza could not dive through them. He
spoke of this, and the others agreed. And through the
trees above, he could see a cliff of yellow rock. Hatta-
zosa liked such places. The others hung back to let him
lead, and followed in single file. Now and then one
would point to a tree at which the hatta-zosa had been
chewing. Then they came to the edge of the brush, to a
stretch of open grass at the foot of the cliff.

There were seven hatta-zosa there, gray beasts as high
at the shoulder as a person's waist, all gnawing at trees.
They wouldn't be able to kill all of them, but if they
killed three or four they would have all the meat they
could eat. By this time, everybody had picked up stones
and carried them nested in the crooks of their elbows.
He touched Lame One with the knob of his killing-club.

"You," he said. "Stonebreaker. Other She. Go back
in brush, come around other side. We wait here. Chase
hatta-zosa to us, kill all you can."

Lame One nodded. He and his companions slipped
away noiselessly. For a long time, Wise One and the
others waited, and then he heard the voice of Lame
One, which the hatta-zosa could not hear: "Watch,
now. We come."

He had a stone in his free hand, ready to throw, when
Lame One and Stonebreaker and Other She burst from
the brush, hurling stones. Other She's stone knocked
down a hatta-zosa and she brained it with her club. A

stone he himself threw dazed another; he threw his other stone, missing, and then ran in, swinging his club. There were shouts all around him and a blur of fast-moving golden-furred bodies. Then it was all over; they had killed four, and three had gotten away. The others wanted to give chase.

"No. We have meat, we eat," he said. "Then we go away, hatta-zosa come back. Next light-time after dark-time, we come back, kill more."

The others hadn't thought that far ahead. That was why they were willing to let Wise One think for them. They all looked around for stones to break to cut up the hatta-zosa, but the stones here were all soft. They would have to use their teeth and fingers. They helped each other, one standing on the neck of a hatta-zosa while two pulled it apart by the hind legs; they used stones as hammers to break the bones.

At first, they ate greedily, for it had been sun-highest time the day before since they had tasted red meat. Then, their hunger satisfied, they ate more slowly, talking about the killing, boasting of what they had done. He found the flat brown thing that was so good, ate half of it, and gave the other half to Little She; the others were also finding and sharing this tidbit.

It was then that he heard the sound of fear, more a rapid vibration in his head than a real noise. The others also heard it, and stopped eating.

"Gotza come," he said. "Two gotza."

They all looked quickly above them, and then began tearing loose meat and cramming their mouths. They would not have long to enjoy this feast. He put up a hand to keep the sun from his eyes, and saw a gotza approaching—the thin body between the wide pointed wings, the pointed head in front, the long tail. It was closer than he liked, and he was sure it had seen them. There was another behind it and, farther away, a third. This was bad.

They all snatched their killing-clubs and the big hind

legs of the hatta-zosa which they had saved for last in
case they might have to run. The first gotza was turning
to dive upon them and they were about to dash under
the trees when the terrible thing happened.

From the top of the cliff above them came a noise,
loud as thunder, but short and hard; he had never heard
a noise like that before. The nearest gotza thrashed its
wings and then fell, straight down. There was a second
noise like the first, but sharper and less loud; the next
gotza also fell, into a tree, crashing down through the
branches. A third noise, exactly like the first, and the
third gotza dropped into the woods. Then was silence.

"Gotza make dead!" somebody cried. "What make
do?"

"Thunder-noise kill gotza; maybe kill us next."

"Bad place this," Lame One was clamoring. "Make
run fast."

They fled, carrying all they could of the meat, back to
the spring. Everything was silent now, except for fright-
cries of birds, also disturbed by the loud noises. Finally
they were still, and there was nothing but the buzzing of
insects. The People began to eat. After a while, there
was a new sound, shrill but not unpleasant. It seemed to
move about, and then grew fainter and went away. The
birds began chirping calmly again.

The People argued while they ate. None of them knew
what had really happened, and most of them wanted to
go as far from this place as they could. Maybe they were
right, but Wise One wanted to know more about what
had happened.

"A new thing has come," he told them. "Nobody has
ever told of a thing like this before. It is a thing that kills
gotza. If it only kills gotza, it is good. If it kills People
too, it is bad. We not know. Better we know now, then
we can take care." He finished gnawing the meat from
the leg-bone and threw it aside, then washed his hands,
dried them on grass, and picked up his club. "Come.
We go back. Maybe we learn something."

The others were afraid, but he was Wise One, One Who Knows Best. If he thought they should go back, that was the thing to do. Sometimes it was good for one to do the thinking for the others. It saved argument, and things got done.

At the foot of the cliff, one gotza lay on the open grass, and feekee-birds had begun to peck at it. That was good; feekee-birds never pecked at anything that had life. They flew away, scolding, as he and the others approached.

There was a small bleeding hole under one of the gotza's wings, as though a sharp stick had been stabbed into it, though he could not see how anything could go through the tough scaly hide. Then he looked at the other side, and gave a cry of astonishment that brought all the others running. Whatever had stabbed the gotza had gone clear through, tearing out a great gaping wound. Maybe it had been thunder that had killed the gotza, though the sky had been blue; he had seen what thunder flashes did when they struck trees. He looked at the other gotza, the one that had fallen through the boughs of the tree. There was a hole under its chin, and the whole top of the head was gone, the skull shattered. He thought of going to look for the third gotza, which had fallen in the woods, but decided not to bother. The others were exchanging shocked comments. Nobody had ever heard of anything being killed like this.

At first, he could persuade none of the others to climb to the top of the cliff, and so started up alone. Before he had reached the top, however, they were all following, ashamed to stay below. There were no trees at the top, only scattered bushes and sparse grass and sandy ground. Everything was still and, until he found the footprints, quite ordinary.

They resembled no footprints any of them had ever seen or heard of; they were a little like the footprints of People, and whatever had made them had walked on two feet. But there were no toe-prints, only a flat sole

that widened at the middle and tapered to a rounded
end, and a heel-mark that looked like the backward
print of some kind of hoof. And they were huge, three
times as big as the footprints of People. Whatever had
made them had walked with a stride longer than a person's height. There were two sets, only slightly different
in size and shape.

He wondered for a moment if they might not have
been made by some kind of giant People. No, that
couldn't be; People were People, and there were no
other kind. At least, nobody had ever told about giant
People. But then, nobody had ever told about something that killed flying gotza with noises like thunder,
either.

Something immense and heavy had rested on the cliff
top not long ago; it had broken bushes and flattened
grass, and even crushed some stones. The strange footprints were all around where it had been. Those who
had made the strange footprints must have brought this
huge and heavy thing with them, and taken it away
again. That meant that they must be very strong indeed.

And it meant that they must be People of some kind.
Only People carried things about with them. One of the
males, the one they called Stabber because he liked to
use the pointed end of his killing-club instead of the
knob, thought of that too.

"Bring big thing here; take away. We look for tracks,
see which way go. Then we go other way."

Stabber didn't wait for Wise One to do all the thinking. He would remember that, teach Stabber all he
knew. Then, if he died, Stabber could lead the band.
They started away from where the heavy thing had
been, to the edge of the cliff. It was there that Little She
found the first of the bright-things.

She cried out and picked it up, holding it out to show.
She should not have done that; she did not know what it
was. But as it had not hurt her, Wise One took it to look
at it. It was not alive, and he did not think it had ever

been, though he could not be sure. There were live-things, things that moved, like People and animals, and live-things that had "made dead." Then there were growing-things, like trees and grass and fruit and flowers; and there were ground-things, stones and rocks and sand and things like that. Usually, one could tell which was which, but not this thing.

It was yellow and bright, and glistened in the sunlight —straight, round through, and a little longer than his hand, open at one end and closed at the other. Near the open end it narrowed abruptly and then became straight again. There was a groove all around the closed end, and in the middle of the closed end was a spot, whitish instead of yellow and dented as though something small and sharp had hit it very hard. Around this spot were odd markings. He sniffed at the open end; it had a sharp, bitter smell, utterly strange.

A moment later Stonebreaker found another, a little smaller and more tapered from the closed end to the shoulder. Then he found a third, exactly like the one Little She had found.

Three thunder-noises, one less loud than the others. Three bright-things, one smaller than the others. And two kinds of bright-things, and two sets of big foot-prints. That might mean something. He would think about it. They found tracks all around where the heavy thing had been, and also to and from the edge of the cliff, but none going away in any direction.

"Maybe fly," Stabber said. "Like bird, like gotza."

"And carry great heavy thing?" Big She asked in-credulously.

"How else?" Stabber insisted. "Come here, go away. Not make tracks on ground, then fly in air."

There was a gotza circling far away; Wise One pointed to it. Soon there would be many gotza, come to feed on the three that had been killed. Gotza ate their own dead; that was another reason why People loathed gotza. Better leave now. Soon the gotza would be close enough to see them. He could hear its wing-sounds very faintly.

Wing-sounds! That was what they had heard at the spring; the shrill, wavering sound had been the wing-sound of the flying Big Ones.

"Yes," he said. "They flew. We heard them."

He looked again at the bright-thing in his hand, comparing it with the other two. Little She was saying:

"Bright-things pretty. We keep?"

"Yes," he told her. "We keep."

Then Wise One looked at the markings on the closed end of the one in his hand. All sorts of things had markings—fruit and stones, and the wings of insects, and the shells of zatku. It was fun to find something with odd markings, and then talk about what they looked like. But nobody ever found anything that was marked:

He didn't wonder what the markings meant. Markings never meant anything. They just happened.

iii.

Jack Holloway signed the paper—authorization for promotion of trooper Felix Krajewski, Zarathustra Native Protection Force, to rank of corporal—and tossed it into the OUT tray. A small breeze, pleasantly cool, came in at the open end of the prefab hut, bringing with it from outside the noises of construction work to compete with the whir and clatter of computers and roboclerks in the main office beyond the partition. He laid down the pen, brushed his mustache with the middle knuckle of his trigger finger, and then picked up his pipe, relighting it. Then he took another paper out of the IN tray.

Authorization for payment of five hundred and fifty sols, compensation for damage done to crops by Fuzzies; endorsed as investigated and approved by George Lunt, Major Commanding, ZNPF. He remembered the incident: a bunch of woods-Fuzzies who had slipped through George's chain of posts at the south edge of the Piedmont and gotten onto a sugar plantation and into mischief. Probably ruined one tenth as many sugarplant seedlings as the land-prawns which the Fuzzies killed there would have destroyed. But the Government wasn't responsible for land-prawns, and it was responsible for Fuzzies, and any planter who wouldn't stick the Government for all the damages he could ought to be stuffed and put in a museum as a unique specimen. He signed it and reached for the next paper.

It was a big one, a lot of sheets stapled together. He pried out the staple. Covering letter from Governor-General Bennett Rainsford, attention Commissioner of Native Affairs; and then another on the letterhead of the Charterless Zarathustra Company, Ltd., of Zarathustra, signed by Victor Grego, Pres. He grinned. That "Charterless" looked like typical Grego gallows humor; it also made sense, since it kept the old initials for the trademark. And for the cattle-brand. Anybody who'd ever tried rebranding a full-grown veldbeest could see the advantage of that.

Acknowledgment of eighteen sunstones, total weight 93.6 carats, removed from Yellowsand Canyon for study prior to signing of lease agreement. Copy of receipt signed by Grego and his chief geologist, endorsed by Gerd van Riebeek, Chief of Scientific Branch, Zarathustra Commission for Native Affairs, and by Lieutenant Hirohito Bjornsen, ZNPF. Color photographs of each of the eighteen stones: they were beautiful, but no photograph could do justice to a warm sunstone, glowing with thermofluorescence. He looked at them carefully. He was an old sunstone-digger himself, and knew what he was looking at. One hundred seventeen thousand sols on the Terra gem market; S-42,120 in royalties for the Government, in trust for the Fuzzies. And this wasn't even the front edge of the beginning; these were just the prospect samples. This time next year . . .

He initialed Ben Rainsford's letter, stapled the stuff together, and tossed it into the FILE tray. As he did, the communication screen beside him buzzed. Turning in his chair, he flipped the screen on and looked, through it, into the interior of another prefab hut like this one, fifteen hundred miles to the north on the Fuzzy Reservation. A young man, with light hair and a pleasantly tough and weather-beaten face, looked out of it. He was in woodsclothes, the breast of his jacket loaded with clips of rifle cartridges.

"Hi, Gerd. What's new?"

Gerd van Riebeek shrugged. "Still sitting on top of 'steen billion sols' worth of sunstones. Victor Grego was up; you heard about that?"

"Yes. I was looking at the photos of those stones a moment ago. How much flint did he have to crack to get them?"

"About seventy-five tons. He took them out from five different locations, on both sides of the canyon. Took him about eight hours, after he got the sandstone off."

"That's better than I ever did; I thought I'd hit it rich when I got one good stone out of six tons of flint. We can tell the Fuzzies they're all rich now."

"They'll want to know if it's good to eat," Gerd said.

They probably would. He asked if Gerd had been seeing many Fuzzies.

"South of the Divide, yes, quite a few in small bands, mostly headed south or southwest. We get more on the movie film than we actually see. North of the Divide, hardly any. Oh, you remember the band we saw the day we found the sunstone flint? The ones who'd killed those goofers and were eating them?"

Holloway laughed, remembering their consternation when the three harpies had put in an appearance and been knocked down by his and Gerd's rifle fire.

" 'Thunder-noise kill gotza; maybe kill us next,' " he quoted. " 'Bad place this, make run fast.' Man, were they a scared lot of Fuzzies."

"They didn't stay scared long; they were back as soon as we were out of there," Gerd told him. "I was up that way this morning and recognized the place; I set down for a look around. The dead harpies were pretty well cleaned up—other harpies and what have you—just a few bones scattered around. I was up on top, where we'd been. It was three weeks ago, and it'd rained a few

times since; so, no tracks. I could hardly see where we'd
set the aircar down. But I know the Fuzzies were there
from what I didn't find.''

Gerd paused, grinning. Expecting Holloway to ask
what.

"The empties, two from my 9.7 and one from your
Sterberg,'' Holloway said. "Sure. Pretty-things.'' He
laughed again. Fuzzies always picked up empty brass.
"You find some Fuzzies with empty cartridges, you'll
know who they are.''

"Oh, they won't keep them. They've gotten tired of
them and dropped them long ago.''

They talked for a while, and finally Gerd broke the
connection, probably to call Ruth. Holloway went back
to his paperwork. The afternoon passed, and eventually
he finished everything they had piled up on him. He rose
stiffly. Wasn't used to this damned sitting on a chair all
day. He refilled and lighted his pipe, got his hat, and
looked for the pistol that should be hanging under it
before he remembered that he wasn't bothering to wear
it around the camp anymore. Then, after a glance
around to make sure he hadn't left anything a Fuzzy
oughtn't to get at, he went out.

They'd built all the walls of the permanent office that
was to replace this hut, and they'd started on the roof.
The ZNPF barracks and headquarters were finished and
occupied; in front of the latter a number of contragravity vehicles were grounded: patrol cars and combat
cars. Some of the former were new, light green with
yellow trim, lettered ZNPF. Some of the latter were
olive green; they and the men who operated them had
been borrowed from the Space Marines. Across the little
stream, he couldn't see his original camp buildings for
the new construction that had gone up in the past two
and a half months; the whole place, marked with a tiny
dot on the larger maps as Holloway's Camp, had been
changed beyond recognition.

Maybe the name ought to be changed, too. Call it

Hoksu-Mitto—that was what the Fuzzies called it—
"Wonderful Place." Well, it *was* pretty wonderful, to a
Fuzzy just out of the big woods; and even those who
went on to Mallorysport, a much more wonderful place,
to live with human families still called it that, and
looked back on it with the nostalgic affection of an old
grad for his alma mater. He'd talk to Ben Rainsford
about getting the name officially changed.

Half a dozen Fuzzies were playing on the bridge; they
saw him and ran to him, yeeking. They all wore zipper-closed shoulder bags, with sheath-knives and little
trowels attached, and silver identity disks at their
throats, and they carried the weapons that had been
issued to them to replace their wooden prawn-killers—
six-inch steel blades on twelve-inch steel shafts. They
were newcomers, hadn't had their vocal training yet; he
put in the earplug and switched on the hearing aid he
had to use less and less frequently now, and they were
all yelling:

"Pappy Jack! Heyo, Pappy Jack. You make play
with us?"

They'd been around long enough to learn that he was
Pappy Jack to every Fuzzy in the place, which as of the
noon count stood at three hundred sixty-two, and they
all thought he had nothing to do but "make play" with
them. He squatted down, looking at their ID-disks; all
numbered in the twelve-twenties, which meant they'd
come in day before yesterday.

"Why aren't you kids in school?" he asked, grabbing
one who was trying to work the zipper of his shirt.

"*Skool*? What is, *skool*?"

"School," he told them, "is place where Fuzzies
learn new things. Learn to make talk like Big Ones, so
Big Ones not need put-in-ear things. Learn to make
things, have fun. Learn not get hurt by Big One things."
He pointed to a long corrugated metal shed across the
run. "School in that place. Come; I show."

He knew what had happened. This gang had met

some Fuzzy in the woods who had told them about Hoksu-Mitto, and they'd come to get in on it. They'd been taken in tow by Little Fuzzy or Ko-Ko or one of George Lunt's or Gerd and Ruth van Riebeek's Fuzzies, and brought to ZNPF headquarters to be fingerprinted and given ID-disks and issued equipment, and then told to go amuse themselves. He started across the bridge, the Fuzzies running beside and ahead of him.

The interior of the long shed was cool and shady, but not quiet. There were about two hundred Fuzzies, all talking at once; when he switched off his hearing aid, most of it was the yeek-yeeking which was the audible fringe sound of their ultrasonic voices. Two of George Lunt's family, named Dillinger and Ned Kelly, were teaching a class—most of whom had already learned to pitch their voices to human audibility—how to make bows and arrows. Considering that they'd only become bowyers and fletchers themselves a month ago, they were doing very well, and the class was picking it up quickly and enthusiastically. His own Mike and Mitzi were giving a class in fire-making, sawing a length of hard wood back and forth across the grain of a softer log. They had a score or so of pupils, all whooping excitedly as the wood-dust began to smoke. Another crowd stood or squatted around a ZNPF corporal who was using a jackknife to skin a small animal Terrans called a zarabunny. Like any good cop, he was continuously aware of everything that went on around him. He looked up.

"Hi, Jack. Soon as that crowd over there have a fire going, I'll show them how to broil this on a stick. Then I'll show them how to use the brains to cure the skin, the way the Old Terran Indians did, and how to make a bowstring out of the gut."

And then, after they'd learned all this stuff, they'd go in to Mallorysport to be adopted by some human family and never use any of it. Well, maybe not. There were a lot of Fuzzies—ten, maybe twenty thousand of them. In spite of what Little Fuzzy was telling everybody about all the Fuzzies having Big Ones of their own, it wouldn't work out that way. There just weren't enough humans who wanted to adopt Fuzzies. So some of this gang would go to the ZNPF posts to the south or along the edge of Big Blackwater to the west, and teach other Fuzzies who'd pass the instruction on. Bows and arrows, fire, cooked food, cured hides. Basketry and pottery, too. Seeing this gang here, it was hard to realize just how primitively woods-Fuzzies had lived. Hadn't even learned to make anything like these shoulder bags to carry things in; had to keep moving all the time, too, hunting and foraging.

Fuzzy sapiens zarathustra—he was glad they'd gotten rid of the *Fuzzy fuzzy holloway* thing; people were beginning to call *him* Fuzzy-Fuzzy—had made one hell of a cultural jump since the evening he'd heard something say, "Yeek," in his shower stall.

Little Fuzzy, across the shed, saw him and waved, and he waved back. Little Fuzzy had a class too, on how to behave among the Big Ones. For a while, he talked with Corporal Carstairs and his pupils. The crowd he'd brought in with him wanted to stay there; he managed to get them away and over to where his own Ko-Ko and Cinderella and the van Riebeeks' Syndrome and Superego were giving vocal lessons.

It had been the Navy people, temporarily sheltering his own family on Xerxes before the Fuzzy trial, who had found out about their ultrasonic voices and made special hearing aids. After the trial, when Victor Grego, once the Fuzzies' archenemy, acquired a Fuzzy of his own and became one of their best friends, he and Henry Stenson, the instrument maker, designed a small self-powered hand-phone Fuzzies could use to transform their voices to audible frequencies. Then Grego discovered that his own Fuzzy, Diamond, was speaking audibly with the power-unit of his Fuzzyphone dead; he had learned to imitate the sounds he had heard himself

making. Diamond was able to teach the trick; now his
pupils were teaching others.

This class had several of the Stenson-Grego Fuzzy-
phones, things with Fuzzy-size pistol grips and grip
switches. They were speaking with them, and then re-
leasing the switches and trying to make the same sounds
themselves. Ko-Ko seemed to be in charge of the instruction.

"No, no!" he was saying. "Not like that. Make talk
away back in mouth, like this."

"Yeek?"

"No. Do again with hold-in-hand thing. Hold tight,
now; make talk."

The van Riebeeks' Syndrome didn't seem to be doing
anything in particular; Holloway spoke to her:

"You make talk to these. Tell about how learn to
make talk like Big Ones." He turned to the Fuzzies who
had come in with him. "You stay here. Do what these
tell you. Soon you make talk like Big Ones too. Then
you come to Pappy Jack, make talk; Pappy Jack give
something nice."

He left them with Syndrome and went over to where
Little Fuzzy sat on a box, smoking his pipe just like
Pappy Jack. A number of the Fuzzies around him, one
of the advanced classes, were also smoking.

"Among Big Ones," he was saying in a mixture of
Fuzzy language and Lingua Terra, "everything belong
somebody. Every place belong somebody. Nobody go
on somebody-else place, take things belong somebody
else."

"No place belong everybody, like woods?" a pupil
asked.

"Oh, yes. Some places. Big Ones have Gov'men'
to take care of places belong everybody. This place,
Hoksu-Mitto, Gov'men' place. Once belong Pappy
Jack; Pappy Jack give to Gov'men', for everybody, all
Big Ones, all Fuzzies."

"But, Gov'men'; what is?"

"Big-One thing. All Big Ones talk together, all pick some for take care of things belong everybody. Gov'-men' not let anybody take somebody-else things, not let anybody make anybody dead, not let hurt anybody. Now, Gov'men' say nobody hurt Fuzzy, make Fuzzy dead, take Fuzzy things. Do this in Big-Room Talk-Place. I saw. Bad Big One make Goldilocks dead; other Big Ones take bad Big One away, make him dead. Then, all say, nobody hurt Fuzzy anymore. Pappy Jack make them do this."

That wasn't exactly what had happened. For instance, Leonard Kellogg had cut his throat in jail, but suicide while of unsound mind was a little complicated to explain to a Fuzzy. Just let it go at that. He strolled on, to where some of George Lunt's family, Dr. Crippen and Lizzie Borden and Calamity Jane, were teaching carpentry, and stayed for a while, watching the Fuzzies using scaled-down saws and augers and drawknives and planes. This crowd was really interested; they'd go out for food after a while and then come back and work far into the evening. They were building a hand-wagon, even the wheels; nearby was a small forge, now cold, and an anvil on which they had made the ironwork.

Finally, he reached the end of the hut where Ruth van Riebeek and Pancho Ybarra, the Navy psychologist on permanent loan to the Colonial Government, sat respectively on a pile of cushions on the floor and the edge of a table. They had a dozen Fuzzies around them.

"Hi, Jack," Ruth greeted him. "When's that husband of mine coming back?"

"Oh, as soon as the agreement's signed and the CZC takes over. How are the kids doing?"

"Oh, we aren't kids anymore, Pappy Jack," Ybarra told him. "We are very grown up. We are graduates, and next week we will be faculty members."

Holloway sat down on the cushions with Ruth, and the Fuzzies crowded around him, wanting puffs from his pipe, and telling him what they had learned and what they were going to teach. Then, by pairs and groups, they drifted away. There was a general breaking-up. The vocal class was dispersing; Syndrome was going away with her group. If she could get them back tomorrow. . . . What this school needed was a truant officer. The fire-making class had gotten a blaze started on the earthen floor, and the butchering-and-cooking class had joined them. The apprentice bowyers and fletchers had already left. Carpentry was still going strong.

"You know, this teaching program," Ruth was saying, "it seems to lack unity."

"She thinks there is a teaching program," Ybarra laughed. "This is still in the trial-and-error—mostly error—stage. After we learn what we have to teach, and how to do it, we can start talking about programs." He became more serious. "Jack, I'm beginning to question the value of a lot of this friction-fire-making, stone-arrowhead, bone-needle stuff. I know they won't all be adopted into human families and most of them will have to live on their own in the woods or in marginal land around settlements, but they'll be in contact with us and can get all the human-made tools and weapons and things they need."

"I don't want that, Pancho. I don't want them made dependent on us. I don't want them to live on human handouts. You were on Loki, weren't you? You know what's happened to the natives there; they've turned into a lot of worthless Native Agency bums. I don't want that to happen to the Fuzzies."

"That's not quite the same, Jack," Ybarra said. "The Fuzzies *are* dependent on us, for hokfusine. They can't get enough of it for themselves."

That was true, of course. The Fuzzies' ancestors had developed, by evolution, an endocrine gland secreting a hormone nonexistent in any other Zarathustran mammal. Nobody was quite sure why; an educated guess was that it had served to neutralize some natural poison in something they had eaten in the distant past. When discovered, a couple of months ago, this hormone had been tagged with a polysyllabic biochemistry name that had been shortened to NFMp.

But about the time Terran humans were starting civilizations in the Nile and Euphrates valleys, the Fuzzies' environment had altered radically. The need for NFMp vanished and, unneeded, it turned destructive. It caused premature and defective, nonviable, births. As a race, the Fuzzies had started dying out. Today, there was only this small remnant left, in the northern wilds of Beta Continent.

The only thing that had saved them from complete extinction had been another biochemical, a complicated long-molecule compound containing, among other things, a few atoms of titanium, which they still obtained by eating land-prawns—zatku, as they called them. And, beginning with their first contacts with humans, they had also gotten it from a gingerbread-colored concoction officially designated Terran Federation Armed Forces Emergency Ration, Extraterrestrial Type Three. Like most synthetic rations, it was loathed by the soldiers and spacemen to whom it was issued, but after the first nibble Fuzzies doted on it. They called it Hoksu-Fusso, "Wonderful Food." The chemical discovered in it, and in land-prawns, had been immediately named hokfusine.

"It neutralizes NFMp, and it inhibits the glandular action that produces it," Ybarra was saying. "But we can't administer it environmentally; we have to supply it to every individual Fuzzy, male and female. Viable births only occur when both parents have gotten plenty of it prior to conception."

The Fuzzies who lived among humans would get plenty of it, but the ones who tried to shift for themselves in the woods wouldn't. The very thing he wanted to avoid, dependence on humans, would be selected for genetically, just as a taste for land-prawns had been. The countdown for the Fuzzy race had been going on for a thousand generations, ten little Fuzzies, nine little Fuzzies, eight little Fuzzies. He didn't know how many more generations until it would be no little Fuzzies if they didn't do something now.

"Don't worry about the next generation, Jack," Ruth said. "Just be glad there'll be one."

iv.

Leslie Coombes laid his cigarette in the ashtray and picked up his cocktail, sipping slowly. As he did so, he gave an irrationally apprehensive glance at the big globe of the planet floating off the floor on its own contragravity, spotlighted by a simulated sun and rotating slowly, its two satellites, Xerxes and Darius, orbiting about it. Darius still belonged outright to the Company, even after the Pendarvis Decisions. Xerxes never had; it had been reserved by the Federation as a naval base when the old Company had been chartered. The evening shadow-line had just touched the east coast of Alpha Continent and was approaching the spot that represented Mallorysport.

Victor Grego caught the involuntary glance and laughed.

"Still nervous about it, Leslie? It's had its teeth pulled."

Yes, after it had been too late, after the Fuzzy Trial, when they had realized that every word spoken in Grego's private office had been known to Naval Intelligence, and that Henry Stenson, who had built it, had been a Federation undercover agent. There had been a microphone and a midget radio transmitter inside. Stenson had planted a similar set in a bartending robot at the Residency, which was why the former Resident General,

Nick Emmert, was now aboard a destroyer bound for
Terra, to face malfeasance charges. Coombes wondered
how many more of those things Stenson had strewn
about Mallorysport; he'd almost dismantled his own
apartment looking in vain for one, and he still wasn't
sure.

"It wouldn't matter, anyhow," Grego continued.
"We're all friends now. Aren't we, Diamond?"

The Fuzzy on Grego's chair-arm snuggled closer to
him, pleased at being included in the Big One conversa-
tion.

"Tha's ri'; everybody friend. Pappy Vic, Pappy
Jack, Unka Less'ee, Unka Gus, Pappy Ben, Flora,
Fauna . . ." He went on naming all the people, Fuzzies
and Big Ones, who were friends. It was a surprising list;
only a few months ago nobody but a lunatic would have
called Jack Holloway and Bennett Rainsford and Gus
Brannhard friends of his and Victor Grego's. "Everybody friend now. Everything nice."

"Everything nice," Coombes agreed. "For the time
being, at least. Victor, you're getting Fuzzy-fuzz all over
your coat."

"Who cares? It's my coat, and it's my Fuzzy, and
besides, I don't think he's shedding now."

"And all bad Big Ones gone to jail-place," Diamond
said. "Not make trouble, anymore. What is like, jail-
place? Is like dark dirty place where bad Big Ones put
Fuzzies?"

"Something like that," Grego told the Fuzzy.

The trouble was, they hadn't put all the bad Big Ones
in jail. They hadn't been able to prove anything against
Hugo Ingermann, and that left a bad taste in his mouth.
And it reminded him of something.

"Did you find the rest of those sunstones, Victor?"

Grego shook his head. "No. At first I thought the
Fuzzies must have lost them in the ventilation system,
but we put robo-snoopers through all the ducts and
didn't find anything. Then Harry Steefer thought some

of his cops had held out on him, but we questioned everybody under veridication and nobody knew anything. I don't know where in Nifflheim they are."

"A quarter-million sols isn't exactly sparrow-fodder, Victor."

"Almost. Wait till we get enough men and equipment in at Yellowsand Canyon; we'll be taking out twice that in a day. My God, Leslie; you ought to see that place! It's fantastic."

"All I'd see would be a lot of rock. I'll take your word for it."

"There's this layer of sunstone flint, averaging two hundred feet thick, all along the face of the Divide for eight and a half miles west of the canyon and better than ten miles east of it; it runs back four miles before it tapers out. Of course, there's a couple of hundred feet of sandstone on top of it that'll have to be stripped off, but we'll just shove that down into the canyon. It won't, really, be as much of a job as draining Big Blackwater was. Are the agreements ready to sign?"

"Yes. The general agreement obligates the Company to continue all the services performed by the old chartered company; in return, the Government agrees to lease us all the unseated public lands declared public domain by the Pendarvis Decisions, except the area north of the Little Blackwater and the north branch of the Snake River, the Fuzzy Reservation. The special agreement gives us a lease on the tract around the Yellowsand Canyon; we pay four-fifty sols for every carat weight of thermofluorescent sunstones we take out, the money to be administered for the Fuzzies by the Government. Both agreements for nine hundred and ninety-nine years."

"Or until adjudged invalid by the court."

"Oh, yes; I got that inserted everywhere I could stick it. The only thing I'm worried about now is how much trouble the Terra-side stockholders of the late Chartered Zarathustra Company may give us."

"Well, they have an equity of some sort, as individuals," Grego admitted. "But there simply is no Chartered Zarathustra Company."

"I can't be positive. The Chartered Loki Company was dissolved by court order, for violation of Federation law. The stockholders lost completely. The Chartered Uller Company was taken over by the Government after the Uprising, in 526; the Government simply confirmed General von Schlichten as governor-general and payed off the stockholders at face value. And when the Chartered Fenris Company went bankrupt, the planet was taken over by some of the colonists, and the stockholders, I believe, were paid two and a quarter centisols on the sol. Those are the only precedents, and none of them apply here." He drank some more of his cocktail. "I shall have to go to Terra myself to represent the new Charterless Zarathustra Company, Ltd., of Zarathustra."

"I'll hate to see you go."

"Thank you, Victor. I'm not looking forward to it, myself." Six months aboard ship would be almost as bad as a jail sentence. And then at least a year on Terra, getting things straightened out and engaging a law firm in Kapstaad or Johannesburg to handle the long litigation that would ensue. "I hope to be back in a couple of years. I doubt if I shall enjoy reaccustoming myself to life on our dear mother planet." He finished what was in his glass and held it up. "May I have another cocktail, Victor?"

"Why, surely." Grego finished his own drink. "Diamond, you please go give Unka Less'ee *koktel-drinko*. Bring *koktel-drinko* for Pappy Vic, too."

"Hokay."

Diamond jumped down from the chair-arm and ran to get the cocktail jug. Leaning forward, Coombes held his glass down where Diamond could reach it; the Fuzzy filled it to the brim without spilling a drop.

"Thank you, Diamond."

"Welcome, Unka Less'ee," Diamond replied just as politely, and carried the jug to fill Pappy Vic's glass.

He didn't pour a drink for himself. He'd had a drink, once, and had never forgotten the hangover it gave him; he didn't want another like it. Maybe that was one of the things Ernst Mallin meant when he said Fuzzies were saner than Humans.

Gustavus Adolphus Brannhard puffed contentedly on his cigar. Behind him, a couple of things more or less like birds twittered among the branches of a tree. In front, the towering buildings of Mallorysport were black against a riot of sunset red and gold and orange. From across the lawn came sounds of Fuzzies—Ben Rainsford's Flora and Fauna and a couple of their visitors—at play. Ben Rainsford, an elfish little man with a bald head and a straggly red beard, sat hunched forward in his chair, staring into a highball he held in both hands.

"But, Gus," he was protesting. "Don't you think Victor Grego can be trusted?"

That was a *volte-face* for Ben. A couple of months ago he'd been positive that there was no infamous treachery too black for Grego.

"Sure I do." Gus shifted the cigar to his left hand and picked up his own drink, an old-fashioned glass full of straight whiskey. "You just have to watch him a little, that's all." A few drops of whiskey dribbled into his beard; he blotted them with the back of his hand and put the cigar back into his mouth. "Why?"

"Well, all this 'until adjudged invalid by the court' stuff in the agreements. You think he's fixing booby traps for us?"

"No. I know what he's doing. He's fixing to bluff the Terra-side stockholders of the old Chartered Company. Make them think he'll break the agreements and negotiate new ones for himself if they don't go along with him. He wants to keep control of the new Company himself.''

"Well, I'm with him on that!" Rainsford said vehemently. "Monopoly or no monopoly, I want the Company run on Zarathustra, for the benefit of Zarathustra. But then, why do you want to hold off on signing the agreements?''

"Just till after the election, Ben. We want our delegates elected, and we want our Colonial Constitution adopted. Once we do that, we won't have any trouble electing the kind of a legislature we want. But there's going to be opposition to this public-land deal. A lot of people have been expecting to get rich staking claims to the land the Pendarvis Decisions put in public domain, and now it's being all leased back to the CZC for a thousand years, and that's longer than any of them want to wait.''

"Gus, a lot more people, and a lot more influential people, are going to be glad the Government won't have to start levying taxes," Rainsford replied.

Ben had a point there. There'd never been any kind of taxation on Zarathustra; the Company had footed all the bills for everything. And now there wouldn't be need for any in the future, not even for the new Native Commission. The Fuzzies would be paying their own way, from sunstone royalties.

"And the would-be land-grabbers aren't organized, and we are," Rainsford went on. "The only organized opposition we ever had was from this People's Prosperity Party of Hugo Ingermann's, and now Ingermann's a dead duck.''

That was overoptimism, a vice to which Ben wasn't ordinarily addicted.

"Ben, any time you think Hugo Ingermann's dead, you want to shoot him again. He's just playing possum.''

"I wish we could have him shot for real, along with the rest of them."

"Well, he wasn't guilty along with the rest of them, that's why we couldn't. It's probably the only thing in his life he hasn't been guilty of, but he didn't know anything about that job till they hauled him in and began interrogating him. Why, Nifflheim, we couldn't even get him disbarred!"

He and Leslie Coombes had tried hard enough, but the Bar Association was made up of lawyers, and lawyers are precedent-minded. Most of them had crooked clients themselves, and most of them had cut corners representing them. They didn't want Ingermann's disbarment used as a precedent against them.

"And now he's defending Thaxter and the Evinses and Novaes," Rainsford said. "He'll get them off, too; you watch if he doesn't."

"Not while I'm Chief Prosecutor!"

He shifted his cigar again, and had a drink on that. He wished he felt as confident as he'd sounded.

The deputy-marshal unlocked the door and stood aside for Hugo Ingermann to enter, looking at him as though he'd crawled from under a flat stone. Everybody was looking at him that way around Central Courts now. He smiled sweetly.

"Thank you, deputy," he said.

"Don't bother, I get paid for it," the uniformed deputy said. "All I hope is they draw my name out of the hat when they take your clients out in the jail-yard. Too bad you won't be going along with them. I'd pay for the privilege of shooting you."

And if he complained to the Colonial Marshal, Max Fane would say, "Hell, so would I."

The steel-walled room was small and bare, its only furnishings a table welded to the steel floor and half a dozen straight chairs. It reeked of disinfectant, like the rest of the jail. He got out his cigarettes and lit one, then laid the box and the lighter on the table and looked quickly about. He couldn't see any screen-pickup—maybe there wasn't any—but he was sure there was a microphone somewhere. He was still looking when the door opened again.

Three men and a woman entered, in sandals, long robes, and, probably, nothing else. They'd been made to change before being brought here, and would change back after a close physical search before being returned to their cells. Another deputy was with them. He said:

"Two hours maximum. If you're through before then, use the bell."

Then the door was closed and locked.

"Don't say anything," he warned. "The room's probably bugged. Sit down; help yourselves to cigarettes."

He remained standing, looking at them: Conrad Evins, small and usually fussy and precise, now tense and haggard. He had been chief gem-buyer for the Company; the robbery had been his idea originally—his or his wife's. Rose Evins, having lighted a cigarette, sat looking at it, her hands on the table. She was a dead woman and had accepted her fate; her face was calm with the resignation of hopelessness. Leo Thaxter, beefy and blue-jowled, with black hair and an out-thrust lower lip, was her brother. He had been top man in the loan-shark racket, and banker for the Mallorysport underworld; and he had been the front through whom Ingermann had acquired title to much of the privately owned real estate north of the city. It had been in one of those buildings, a vacant warehouse, that the five Fuzzies captured on Beta Continent had been kept and trained to crawl through ventilation ducts and remove simulated sunstones from cabinets in a mock-up of the Company gem-vault. Phil Novaes, the youngest of the four, was afraid and trying not to show it. He and his partner, Moses Herckerd, former Company survey-scouts, had captured the Fuzzies and brought them to town. Herckerd wasn't present; he'd stopped too many submachine-gun bullets the night of the attempted robbery.

"Well," he began when he had their attention, "they have you cold on the larceny and burglary and criminal conspiracy charges. Nobody, not even I, can get you acquitted of them. That's ten-to-twenty, and don't expect any minimum sentences, either; they'll throw the book at all of you. I do not, however, believe that you can be convicted of the two capital charges—enslavement and faginy. Just to make sure, though, I believe it would be wise for you to plead guilty to the larceny and burglary and conspiracy charges if the prosecution will agree to drop the other two."

The four looked at one another. He lit a fresh cigarette from the end of the old one, dropping the butt on the floor and tramping it.

"Twenty years is a hell of a long time," Thaxter said. "You're dead a damn sight longer, though. Yes, if you can make a deal, go ahead."

"What makes you think you can?" Conrad Evins demanded. "You say they're sure of conviction on the sunstone charges. Why would they take a plea on them and drop the Fuzzy charges? That's what they really want to convict us on."

"Want to, yes. But I don't believe they can, and I think Gus Brannhard doesn't, either. Enslavement is the reduction of a sapient being to the status of chattel property; purchase or sale of a sapient being so chattelized; and/or compulsory labor or service under restraint. Well, we'll claim those Fuzzies weren't slaves but willing accomplices."

"That's not the way the Fuzzies tell it," Rose Evins said indifferently.

"In court, the Fuzzies won't tell it any way at all," he told them. "In court, the Fuzzies will not be permitted to testify. Take my word for it; they just won't."

"Well, that's good news," Thaxter grunted skeptically. "If true. How about the faginy charge?"

Ingermann puffed on his cigarette and blew smoke at the overhead light, then sat down on the edge of the table. "Faginy," he began, "consists of training minor children to perform criminal and/or immoral acts; and/or compelling minor children to perform such acts; and/or deriving gain or profit from performance of such acts by minor children. According to the Pendarvis Decisions, Fuzzies are legally equivalent to human children of under twelve years of age, so according to the Pendarvis Decisions, what you did when you trained those Fuzzies to crawl through ventilation ducts and remove simulated sunstones from cabinets in a mock-up of the Company gem-vault was faginy; and so was taking them to Company House and having them crawl in and get out the real sunstones; and, according to law, the penalty is death by shooting—mandatory and without discretion of the court.

"Well, I'm attacking this legal fiction that a mature adult Fuzzy is a minor child. No one in this Government-Company axis wants to have to defend the Fuzzies' minor-child status in court. That's why they'll take your pleas on the sunstone charges and drop the Fuzzy charges. As you remarked, Leo, twenty years is a long time, but you're dead a lot longer."

An incredulous, almost hopeful, look came into Rose Evins's eyes, and was instantly extinguished. She wasn't going to abandon the peace of resignation for the torments of hope.

"Well, yes," she said softly. "Plead us guilty on those other charges. It won't make any difference."

Her husband also agreed, taking his cue from her; Novaes took his from both, simply nodding. Thaxter's mouth curved down more at the corners, and his lower lip jutted out farther.

"It better not," he said. "Ingermann, if you plead us

guilty on the sunstone charges and then get us shot for faginy or enslavement—"

"Shut up!" Ingermann barked. He was frightened; he knew what Thaxter was going to say next. "You damned fool, didn't I tell you they have this room bugged?"

V.

Wise One woke in the dawn chill; Little She and Big She and Lame One and Fruitfinder were cuddled against him, warmed by his body heat as he was by theirs. Lame One, waking, stirred. It was still dark under the thorn-bushes, but there was a faint grayness above; the sun was stirring awake in its sleeping-place, too, and would soon come out to make light and warmth. The others, Stonebreaker and Stabber and Other She, were also waking. This had been a good sleeping-place, safe and cozy. It would be nice to lie here for a long time, but soon they would have to relieve themselves, and that would mean digging holes. And he was hungry. He said so, and the others agreed.

Little She said: "Don't leave pretty bright-things. Take along."

They would take them, and, as usual, Little She would carry them. Lately the others had begun calling her Carries-Bright-Things. But they all wanted to keep them. They were pretty and strange, and they never tired of looking at them and talking about them and playing with them. Once, they lost one of the bigger ones, and they had gone back and hunted for it from before sun-highest time until a long while after before they found it. After that, they had broken off three sticks and wedged one into the open end of each bright-

thing, so that they would be easier to carry and harder
to lose.

The daylight grew stronger; birds twittered happily.
They found soft ground and dug their holes. They
always did that—bury the bad smells, even if they went
away at once. Then they went to the little stream and
drank and splashed in it, and then waded across and
started, line-abreast, to hunt. The sky grew bright blue,
flecked with golden clouds. He wondered again about
the sleeping-place of the sun, and why the sun always
went into it from one part of the sky and came out from
another. The People had argued about that for as long
as he could remember, but nobody really knew why.

They found a tree with round fruit on it. When best,
this kind of fruit was pure white. Now it was spotted
with brown and was not so good, but they were hungry.
They threw sticks to knock it down, and ate. They
found and ate lizards and grubs. Then they found a
zatku.

Zatku were hard-shelled things, as long as an arm,
with many legs, a hand and one finger of legs on each
side, and four jointed arms ending in sharp jaws. Zatku
could hurt with these; it had been a zatku that had hurt
Lame One's leg. Stonebreaker poked this one with the
sharp end of his killing-club, and it grasped it with all
four jaw-arms. Immediately, Other She stamped the
knob of her club down on its head and, to make sure,
struck again. Then they all stood back while Wise One
broke and tore away the shell and pulled off one of the
jaw-arms to dig out the meat. They all trusted him to see
that everybody got a share. There was enough that
everybody could have a second small morsel.

They hunted for a long time, and found another
zatku. This was good; it had been a long time since they
had found two zatku in one day. They hunted outward
after they had eaten the second one, until almost sun-
highest time, but they did not find any more.

They found other things to eat, however. They found

the soft pink growing-things, like hands with many fingers; they were good. They killed one of the fat little animals with brown fur that ran from one of them and was clubbed by another. And Stonebreaker threw his club and knocked down a low-flying bird; everyone praised him for that. As they hunted they had been climbing the slope of a hill. By the time they reached the top, everybody had found enough to eat.

The hilltop was a nice place. There were a few trees and low bushes and stretches of open grass, and from it they could see a long way. Far to sun-upward, a big river wound glinting through the trees, and there were mountains all around. It was good to lie in the soft grass, warmed by the sun, the wind ruffling their fur and tickling pleasantly.

There was a gotza circling in the sky, but it was too far away to see them. They sat and watched it; once it made a short turn, one wing high, then dived down out of sight.

"Gotza see something," Stonebreaker said. "Go down, eat."

"Hope not People," Big She said.

"Not many People this place," he said. "Long time not see other People."

It had been many-many days ago, far to the sun's right hand, that they had last talked to other People, a band of two males and three females. They had talked a long time and made sleeping-place together, and the next day they had parted to hunt. They had not seen those People again. Now they talked about them.

"We see again, we show bright-things," Lame One said. "Nobody ever see bright-things before."

The gotza rose again, and they could hear its wing-sounds now. It began soaring in wide circles, coming closer.

"Not eat long," Stabber commented. "Something little. Still hungry."

Maybe they had better leave this place now and go

down where the trees were thicker. Wise One was about
to speak of that, and then he heard the shrill, not unpleasant, sound they had heard at the spring after the
thunder-death had killed those three gotza. He recognized it at once; so did the others.

"Get under bushes," he commanded. "Lie still."

There was a tiny speck in the sky, far to the sun's left
hand; it grew larger very rapidly, and the sound grew
louder. He noticed that the sound was following behind
it, and wondered why that was. Then they were all
under the bushes, lying very still.

It was an odd thing to be flying. It had no wings. It
was flattish, rounded in front and pointed behind, like
the seed of a melon-fruit, and it glistened brightly. But
there were no flying Big Ones carrying it; it was flying of
itself.

It flew straight at the gotza, passing almost directly
over them. The gotza turned and tried desperately to
escape, but the flying thing closed rapidly upon it. Then
there was a sound, not the sharp crack of the thunder-
death, but a ripping sound. It could be many thunder-
death sounds close together. It lasted two heartbeats,
and then the gotza came apart in the air, pieces flying
away and falling. The strange flying thing went on for a
little, turning slowly and coming back.

"Good thing, kill gotza," Stabber said. "Maybe see
us, kill gotza so gotza not kill us. Maybe friend."

"Maybe kill gotza for fun," Big She said. "Maybe
kill us next, for fun."

It was coming straight toward them now, lower and
more slowly than when it had chased the gotza. Carries-
Bright-Things and Fruitfinder wanted to run; Wise One
screamed at them to lie still. One did not run from
things like this. Still, he wanted to run himself, and it
took all his will to force himself to lie motionless.

The front of the flying thing was open. At least, he
could see into it, though there was a queer shine there.
Then he gasped in amazement. Inside the flying thing

were two big People. Not People like him, but People of some kind. They had People faces, with both eyes in front, and not one on each side like animal faces. They had People hands, but their shoulders were covered with something strange that was not fur.

So these were the flying Big Ones. They had no wings; when they wanted to fly, they got into the melon-seed-shaped thing, and it flew for them, and when it came down on the ground, they got out and walked about. Now he knew what the great heavy thing that had broken bushes and crushed stones under it had been. It might be some live-thing that did what the Big Ones wanted it to, or it might be some kind of a made-thing. He would have to think more about that. But the Big Ones were just big People.

The flying thing passed over them and was going away; the shrill wavering sound grew fainter, and it vanished. The Big Ones in it had seen them, and they had not let loose the thunder-death. Maybe the Big Ones knew that they were People too. People did not kill other People for fun. People made friends with other People, and helped them.

He rose to his feet. The others, rising with him, were still frightened. So was he, but he must not let them know it. Wise One should not be afraid. Stabber was less afraid than any of the rest; he was saying:

"Big Ones see us, not kill. Kill gotza. Big Ones good."

"You not know," Big She disputed. "Nobody ever know about Big Ones flying before."

"Big Ones kill gotza to help us," he said. "Big Ones make friends."

"Big Ones make thunder-death, make us all dead like gotza," Stonebreaker insisted. "Maybe Big Ones come back. We go now, far-far, then they not find us."

They were all crying out now, except Stabber. Big She and Stonebreaker were loudest and most vehement. They did not know about the Big Ones; nobody had ever told of Big Ones; nobody knew anything about them. They were to be feared more than gotza. There was no use arguing with them now. He looked about, over the country visible from the hilltop. The big moving-water to sun-upward was too wide to cross; he had seen it. There were small moving-waters flowing into it, but they could follow to where the water was little enough to cross over. He pointed toward the sun's left hand with his club.

"We go that way," he said. "Maybe find zatku."

Through the armor-glass front of the aircar, Gerd van Riebeek saw the hilltop tilt away and the cloud-dappled sky swing dizzily. He lifted his thumb from the button-switch of the camera and reached for his cigarettes on the ledge in front of him.

"Make another pass at them, Doc?" the ZNPF trooper at the controls asked.

He shook his head.

"Uh-uh. We scared Nifflheim out of them as it is; don't let's overdo it." He lit a cigarette. "Suppose we swing over to the river and circle around along both sides of it. We might see some more Fuzzies."

He wasn't optimistic about that. There weren't many Fuzzies north of the Divide. Not enough land-prawns. No zatku, no hokfusine; no hokfusine, no viable births. It was a genetic miracle there were any at all up here. And even if the woods were full of them, with their ultrasonic hearing they'd hear the vibrations of an aircar's contragravity field and be under cover before they could be spotted.

"We might see another harpy." Trooper Art Parnaby had been a veldbeest herder on Delta Continent before he'd joined the Protection Force; he didn't have to be taught not to like harpies. "Man, you took that one apart nice!"

Harpies were getting scarce up here. Getting scarce all over Beta. They'd vanished from the skies of the cattle country to the south, and the Company had chased them out or shot them up in the Big Blackwater, and now the ZNPF was working on them in the reservation. As a naturalist, he supposed that he ought to deplore the extinction of any species, but he couldn't think of a better species to become extinct than *Pseudopterodactyl harpy zarathustra*. They probably had their place in the overall ecological picture—everything did. Scavengers, maybe, though they preferred live meat. Elimination of weak and sickly individuals of other species—though any veldbeest herder like Art Parnaby would tell you that no harpy would bother a sick cow if he could land on a plump and healthy calf.

"I wonder if that's the same gang you and Jack saw the time you found the sunstones," Parnaby was saying.

"Could be. There were eight in that gang; I'm sure there were that many in this one. That was a couple of hundred miles north of here, but it was three weeks ago."

The car swung lower; it was down to a couple of hundred feet when they passed over the Yellowsand River, which was broad and sluggish here, with sandbars and sandy beaches. He saw a few bits of brush with half-withered leaves, stuff carried down from where Grego and his gang had been digging a week ago at the canyon. Tributary streams flowed in from both sides, some large enough to be formidable barriers to Fuzzies. Fuzzies could swim well enough, and he'd seen them crossing streams clinging to bits of driftwood; but they didn't like to swim, and didn't when it wasn't necessary. Usually, they'd follow a stream up to where it was small enough to wade across.

They saw quite a few animals. Slim, deerlike things with three horns; there were a dozen species of them, but everybody called all of them, indiscriminately, zarabuck. Fuzzies called them all *takku*. Once he saw a big three-horned damnthing, *hesh-nazza* in Fuzzy language;

he got a few feet of it on film before it saw the car and bolted. Now, there was a poor mixed-up critter; originally a herbivore, it had acquired a taste for meat but couldn't get enough to support the huge bulk of its body, and had to supplement its diet with browse. The whole zoological picture on this planet was crazy. That was why he liked Zarathustra.

They came to where Lake-Chain River joined Yellowsand. At its mouth, it was larger than the stream it fed, and it came in from almost due south, while the Yellowsand, which rose in the Divide, curved in from the east. Beyond this, there weren't any sandbars. The current was more rapid, and the water foamed whitely around bare rocks. The wall of the Divide began looming on the horizon. Finally they could see the cleft of the canyon. There was a circling dot in the sky ahead, but it wasn't a harpy. It was one of the CZC air-survey cars, photomapping and measuring with radar, and scanning. He looked at his watch. Almost 1700, getting on to cocktail time. He wondered how many Fuzzies Lieutenant Bjornsen had seen on his sweep south of the Divide, and how many harpies he'd shot.

vi.

The Fuzzies had been excited all the way from Hoksu-Mitto; Pappy Jack was taking them on a trip to Big House Place. By the time Mallorysport came up on the horizon, tall buildings towering out of green inter-spaces, they were all shrieking in delight, some even for-getting to "make talk in back of mouth," like Big Ones. They came in over the city at five thousand feet, the car slanting downward, and Little Fuzzy recognized Com-pany House at once.

"Look! Diamond Place! Pappy Jack, we go there, see Diamond, Pappy Vic?"

"No, we go Pappy Ben Place," he told them. "Pappy Vic, Diamond, come there. Have big party; every-body come. Pappy Ben, Flora, Fauna, Pappy Vic, Dia-mond . . ." The Fuzzies all added more names of friends they would see. "And look." He pointed to Central Courts Building, on the right. "You know that place?"

They did; that was Big-Room Talk-Place. They'd had a lot of fun there, turning a court trial into a three-ring circus. He still had to laugh when he remembered that. The aircar circled in toward Government House. Un-like the other important buildings of Mallorysport, it sprawled instead of towering, terraced on top, with gar-dens spread around it. On the north lower lawn a crowd of Fuzzies and others were gathered in the loose concen-

tration of an outdoor cocktail party. Then the car was
landing and the Fuzzies were all trying to get out as soon
as it was off contragravity.

There was a group at the foot of the north escalator.
Most of them were small people with golden fur—Ben
Rainsford's Flora and Fauna, Victor Grego's Diamond,
Judge and Mrs. Pendarvis's Pierrot and Columbine,
and five Fuzzies whose names were Allan Pinkerton and
Arsene Lupin and Sherlock Holmes and Irene Adler and
Mata Hari. They were members of the Company Police
Detective Bureau, and they were all reformed criminals.
At least, they had been apprehended while trying to
clean out the gem-vault at Company House and had
turned people's evidence on the gang who had trained
them to be burglars.

With them was a tall girl with coppery hair, and a
dark-faced man whose smartly tailored jacket bulged
slightly under the left arm. The man was Ahmed Khadra, Detective-Captain, in charge of the Native Protection Force, Investigation Division. The girl was Sandra
Glenn, Victor Grego's Fuzzy-sitter. Grego was just
losing her to Khadra, if the sunstone on her left hand
meant anything.

His own Fuzzies had dashed down the escalator ahead
of him; the ones below ran forward to greet them. He
managed to get through the crowd to Ahmed and
Sandra, and had a few words with them before all the
Fuzzies came pelting up, Diamond and Flora and Fauna
and the others tugging at his trouser-legs and wanting
to be noticed, and his own Fuzzies wanting Unka
Ahmed and Auntie Sandra to notice them. He
squatted among them, petting them and saying hello.
Baby Fuzzy promptly climbed onto Ahmed Khadra's
shoulder. At least they'd broken him of trying to sit on
people's heads, which was something. Between talking
to the Fuzzies, all of whom wanted to be talked to, he
managed to get a few more words with Ahmed and San-

dra, mostly about the Fuzzy Club she was going to manage.

"It's going to be just one big nonstop Fuzzy party all the time," she said. "I hope we don't get too tired of it."

It was Victor Grego's idea; he was putting up the money and providing the lower floors and surrounding parkland of one of the Company buildings. People who'd adopted Fuzzies couldn't be expected to give them their exclusive attention, and Fuzzies living with human families would want to talk to and play with other Fuzzies. The Fuzzy Club would be a place where they could get together and be kept out of danger and/or mischief.

"When's the grand opening? I'll have to come in for it."

"Oh, not for a few weeks. After Ahmed and I are married. We still have a lot of fixing up to do, and I want the girl who's taking my place with Diamond to get better acquainted with him, and vice versa, before I leave her to cope with him alone."

"You need much coping with?" he asked Diamond, rumpling his fur and then smoothing it again.

"Actually, no; he's very good. The girl will have to learn more about him, is all. He's being a big help with the Fuzzy Club; gives all sorts of advice, some of it excellent."

Diamond had been telling Little Fuzzy and the others about the new Fuzzy Place. The five ex-jewel-thieves had gotten Baby Fuzzy away from Khadra and were making a great to-do over him, to Mamma's proud pleasure. Ko-Ko and Cinderella and Mike and Mitzi had wandered away somewhere with Pierrot and Columbine. Little Fuzzy was tugging at him.

"Pappy Jack? Little Fuzzy go with Flora, Fauna?" he asked.

"Sure. Run along and have fun. Pappy Jack go make

talk with other Big Ones." He turned to Ahmed and Sandra. "Don't you folks want *koktel-drinko*?"

"We had," Ahmed said. Sandra added, "We have to see about dinner for Fuzzy-people pretty soon."

He said he'd see them around, and strolled away, filling his pipe, toward the crowd around the bartending robot. Diamond accompanied him, mostly in short dashes ahead and waits for him to catch up; what was the matter with Big Ones, anyhow, always poking along? There was an approaching bedlam, and three Fuzzies burst into sight, blowing horns. Behind them, in single file, came three small wheelbarrows, a Fuzzy pushing and another riding in each, with more Fuzzies dashing along behind.

"Look, Pappy Jack! Whee'barrow!" Diamond called. "Pappy Ben give. Fun. Unka Ahmed, Auntie Sandra, they have whee'barrow at new Fuzzy Place."

The procession came to a disorderly halt a hundred yards beyond; the Fuzzies pushing dropped the shafts and took the places of the three who had been riding; three more picked up the wheelbarrows, and the whole cavalcade dashed away again.

"Good little fellows," somebody behind him said. "Everybody takes his fair turn."

The speaker was Associate-Justice Yves Janiver, with silver-gray hair and a dramatically black mustache; he was now presiding judge of Native Cases court. One of his companions was big and ruddy, Clyde Garrick, head cashier of the Bank of Mallorysport. The other, thin and elderly, with a fringe of white hair under a black beret, was Henry Stenson, the instrument-maker. Holloway greeted and shook hands with them.

"Those were my three who just jumped off," Stenson said.

He'd gotten them on loan from the Adoption Bureau, to help test the voice-transformer he and Grego had invented. Then the Fuzzies had refused to go back, and he'd had to adopt them; they'd adopted him already.

Their names were Microvolt and Roentgen and Angstrom. Damned names some people gave Fuzzies. He asked how they were getting along.

"Oh, they're having a wonderful time, Mr. Holloway," Stenson laughed. "I've fixed them up a little workshop of their own, to keep them out of everybody's way in my shop. They want to help everybody do everything; I never saw anybody as helpful as those Fuzzies. You know," he added, "they are a help, too. They have almost microscopic vision, and they're wonderfully clever with their hands." From Henry Stenson, that was high praise. "Well, they're small people; they live on a smaller scale than we do. If only they didn't lose interest so quickly. When they do, of course, it's no use expecting them to go on."

"No, it isn't fun anymore. Besides, they don't understand what you want them to do, or why."

"No, they wouldn't," Stenson agreed. "Explaining a micromass detector or a radiation counter to a Fuzzy . . ." He thought for a moment. "I think I'll start them on jewelry work. They like pretty things, and they'd make wonderful jewelers."

That was an idea. Maybe, about a year from now, an exhibition of Fuzzy arts and handcrafts. Talk that over with Gerd and Ruth; talk it over with Little Fuzzy and Dr. Crippen, too.

A dozen Fuzzies rushed past—the five Company Police Fuzzies and Mamma Fuzzy with Baby running beside her, and some others he felt he ought to know but didn't. They were all swirling around a big red-and-gold ball, rolling it rapidly on the grass. Diamond took off after them.

"Why don't you teach them some real ball games, Jack?" Clyde Garrick asked. He was a sports enthusiast. "Football, now; a Fuzzy football game would be something to watch." A Fuzzy directly in front of the rolling ball leaped over it, coming down among those who were pushing it. "Basketball; did you see the jump that one made? I wish I could get a team of human kids who could jump like that together.''·

Holloway shook his head. "Some of the marines out at Hoksu-Mitto tried to teach them soccer,'' he said. "Didn't work, at all. They couldn't see the sense of the rules, and they couldn't understand why all of them couldn't play on both teams. If a Fuzzy sees somebody trying to do something, all he wants to do is help.''

That shocked Garrick. He didn't think people who lacked competitive spirit were people at all. Stenson nodded.

"What I was saying. They want to help everybody. You could interest them in the sort of sports in which one really competes with oneself. If you teach a Fuzzy something new, he isn't satisfied till he can do it again better.''

"Rifle shooting,'' Garrick grudged. He didn't consider shooting a sport at all. Not an athletic sport, at any rate. "I know shooters who claim they get just as much fun shooting alone as in a match.''

"I don't know about that. A Fuzzy would need an awfully light rifle and awfully light loads. Mind, they only weigh fifteen or twenty pounds. A .22 light enough for a Fuzzy to handle would kick him as hard as my 12.7 express kicks me. But archery'd be all right. We've been teaching them to make bows and arrows and shoot them. You'd be surprised; most of them can pull a twenty-pound bow; and for them that's heavier than a hundred-pound bow for a man.''

"Huh!'' Garrick looked at the swirl of golden bodies around the bright-colored ball. Anybody who weighed so little and could pull a twenty-pound bow deserved respect, team spirit or no team spirit. "Tell you what, Jack. I'll put up cups for regional archery matches and for a world's championship match, and we can start having matches and organizing teams. Say, in a year, we could hold a match for the world's title.''

What a Fuzzy would do with a trophy cup now!

"But what I'd really like to see," Garrick continued, "would be a real live Fuzzy football league. Don't you think you could get some interest stirred up?"

No, and a damned good thing. Start Fuzzy football, and the gamblers would be onto it like a Fuzzy after a land-prawn. And from what he knew about Fuzzies, any Fuzzy could be fixed to throw a game for half a cake of Extee Three; and everybody on both teams would help, just to do what some Big One wanted. No, no Fuzzy football.

While he had been talking he had been edging and nudging the others toward the bartending robot. Yves Janiver, whose glass was empty, was aiding and abetting. As soon as they were close enough, he and the Native Court judge stepped in to get drinks. He was being supplied with his when he was greeted by Claudette Pendarvis, who asked if he had just arrived.

"Practically. I saw your two; they're off somewhere with some of mine," he said. "Is the judge here yet?"

No; he wasn't. She asked Janiver if he knew where the Chief Justice was. In conference, in chambers—he and Gus Brannhard and some other lawyers. Pendarvis and Brannhard would be arriving a little later. Mrs. Pendarvis wanted to know if he was going to visit Adoption Bureau while he was in town.

"Yes, surely, Mrs. Pendarvis. Tomorrow morning be all right?"

Tomorrow morning would be fine. He asked her how things were going. Adoptions, she said, had fallen off somewhat; that was what he'd been expecting.

"But the hospital wants some more Fuzzies, to entertain the patients. They have some now; they want more. And Dr. Mallin says they are a wonderful influence on some of the mental patients."

"Well, we can use some more at school," a woman who had just come up said—Mrs. Hawkwood, principal of the kindergarten and primary schools. "We have a couple already, in the preliterate classes. Do you know, the Fuzzies are actually teaching the human children?''

Age-group four to six; yes, he could believe that.

"Why just preliterates, Mrs. Hawkwood?" he asked.
"Put some of them into the c-a-t-spells-cat class and see
how fast they pick it up. Bet they do better than the
human six year olds."

"You mean, try to teach *Fuzzies* to *read*?"

The idea had never occurred to him before; it seemed
like a good one. Evidently it hadn't occurred to Mrs.
Hawkwood, either, and now that it was presented to
her, he could almost watch her thoughts chase one another across her face. Teach Fuzzies to read? Ridiculous; only people could read. But Fuzzies were people;
there was scientific authority for that. But they were
Fuzzies; that was different. But then . . .

At that point, Ben Rainsford came up, apologetic for
not having greeted him earlier and asking if his family
had come in with him. While he was talking to Ben,
Holloway saw Chief Justice Pendarvis and Gus Brannhard approach. The Chief Justice got a glass of wine for
himself and a cocktail for his wife; they stepped aside
together. Brannhard, big and bearded and giving the
impression, in spite of his meticulous courtroom black,
of being in hunting clothes, secured a tumbler of
straight whiskey. Victor Grego and Leslie Coombes
came up and spoke. Then somebody pulled Rainsford
aside to talk to him.

That was the trouble with these cocktail parties. You
met everybody and never had a chance to talk to anybody. It was getting almost that bad at cocktail time out
at Hoksu-Mitto now. Out of the corner of his eye, Holloway saw Mrs. Hawkwood fasten upon Ernst Mallin.
Mallin was a real authority on Fuzzy psychology; if he
told her Fuzzies could be taught to read, she'd have to
believe it. He wanted to talk to Ernst himself about that,
and about a lot of other things, but not in this donny-
brook.

The wheelbarrow parade came by, more slowly and

less noisily, and a little later the crowd that had been
chasing the big ball came pushing it along, Baby Fuzzy
jumping onto it and tumbling off it. Dinnertime for
Fuzzies—putting back all the playthings where they belonged. He was in favor of using Fuzzies in schools for
human children; maybe they'd have a civilizing influence. After a while, the Fuzzies came stringing back,
mostly talking about food.

Dinnertime for Big Ones, too. It took longer to get
them mobilized than it had the Fuzzies, and then, of
course, they had to stop on the upper terrace where
Sandra Glenn and Ahmed Khadra and some of the Government House staff had set up a Fuzzy-type smorgas-
bord on a big revolving table. The Fuzzies all thought
that was fun. So did the human-people watching them.
Eventually, they all got into the dining room. There
weren't enough ladies to pair off the guests, male and
female after their kind like the passengers on the Ark.
They placed Jack Holloway between Ben Rainsford and
Leslie Coombes, with Victor Grego and Gus Brannhard
on the other side.

By the time the robo-service in the middle of the table
had taken away the dessert dishes and brought in coffee
and liqueurs, Fuzzies were beginning to filter in. They'd
finished their own dinner long ago; it was getting dark
outside, and they wanted to be where the Big Ones were.
Couldn't blame them; it was their party, wasn't it? They
came in diffidently, like well-brought-up children, looking but not touching anything, saying hello to people.

Diamond came over to Grego, who picked him up
and set him on the edge of the table. Rainsford pushed
back his chair, and Flora and Fauna climbed onto his
lap. Gus Brannhard had four or five trying to clamber
over him. Little Fuzzy wanted up on the table, too, and
promptly unzipped his pouch, got out his little pipe, and
lighted it. Several came to Leslie Coombes, begging,
"Unka Less'ee, plis give smokko?" and Coombes lit
cigarettes for them. Coombes liked Fuzzies, and treated

them with the same grave courtesy he showed his human
friends, but he didn't want them climbing over him, and
they knew it.

"Ben, let's get these agreements signed," Grego said.
"Then we can give the kids some attention."

"Where'll we sign them, in your office?" he asked
Rainsford.

"No, sign them right here at the table where everybody can watch. That's what the party's about, isn't
it?" Rainsford said.

They cleared a space in front of the Governor-General, putting Fuzzies on the floor or handing them to
people farther down on either side. The scrolls, three
copies of each agreement, were brought; Rainsford had
one of his secretaries read them aloud. The first was the
general agreement, by which the Colonial Government
agreed to lease, for nine hundred and ninety-nine years,
all unseated public lands to the Charterless Zarathustra
Company, Ltd., of Zarathustra, excepting the area on
Beta Continent set aside as a Fuzzy Reservation, in
return for which the said Charterless Zarathustra Company, Ltd., agreed to carry on all the nonprofit public
services previously performed by the Chartered Zarathustra Company, and, in addition, to conduct re-
searches and studies for the benefit of the race known as
Fuzzy sapiens zarathustra at Science Center. Except for
the northern part of Beta Continent, the new Company
was getting back, as lessees, everything it had lost as
owner by the Pendarvis Decisions.

Rainsford and Grego signed it, with Gus Brannhard
and Leslie Coombes as cosigners, with a few witnesses
chosen at random from around the table. Then the Yellowsand Canyon agreement was read; as commissioner
of Native affairs, Holloway had an interest in that. The
Company leased, also for nine hundred ninety-nine
years, a tract fifty miles square around the head of
Yellowsand Canyon, with rights to mine, quarry, erect
buildings, and remove from the tract sunstones and

other materials. The Government agreed to lease other tracts to the Company, subject to the consent of the Native Commission, and to lease land on the Fuzzy Reservation to nobody else without consent of the Company. The Company agreed to pay royalties on all sunstones removed, at the rate of four hundred fifty sols per carat, said moneys to be held in trust for the Fuzzies as a race by the Colonial Government and invested with the Banking Cartel, the interest accruing to the Government as an administration fee. Well, that put the Government in the black, and made the Fuzzies rich, and gave the Charterless Zarathustra Company more than the Chartered Zarathustra Company had lost. Everybody ought to be happy.

Rainsford and Grego, and Gus and Leslie Coombes signed it, so did Jack Holloway, as Commissioner of Native Affairs. They picked half a dozen more witnesses who also signed.

"What's the matter with having a few Fuzzies sign it too?" Grego asked, indicating the crowd that had climbed to the table on both sides to watch what the Big Ones were doing. "It's their Reservation, and it's their sunstones."

"Oh, Victor," Coombes protested. "They can't sign this. They're incompetent aborigines, and legally minor children. And besides, they can't write. At least, not yet."

"They can fingerprint after their names, the way any other illiterates do," Gus Brannhard said. "And they can sign as additional witnesses; neither as aborigines nor as minor children are they debarred from testifying to things of their own experience or observation. I'm going to send Leo Thaxter and the Evinses and Phil Novaes out to be shot on Fuzzy testimony."

"Chief Justice Pendarvis, give us a guidance-opinion on that," Coombes said. "I'd like some Fuzzies to sign it, but not if it would impair the agreement."

"Oh, it would not do that, Mr. Coombes," Pendarvis

said. "Not in my opinion, anyhow. Mr. Justice Janiver, what's your opinion?"

"Well, as witnesses, certainly," Janiver agreed. "The Fuzzies are here present and the signing takes place within their observation; they can certainly testify to that."

"I think," Pendarvis said, "that the Fuzzies ought to be informed of the purpose of this signing, though."

"Mr. Brannhard, you want to try that?" Coombes asked. "Can you explain the theory of land-tenure, mineral rights, and contractual obligation in terms comprehensible to a Fuzzy?"

"Jack, you try it; you know more about Fuzzies than I do," Brannhard said.

"Well, I can try." He turned to Diamond and Little Fuzzy and Mamma Fuzzy and a few others closest to him.

"Big Ones make name-marks on paper," he said. "This means, Big Ones go into woods—place Fuzzies come from—dig holes, get stones, make trade with other Big Ones. Then get nice things, give to Fuzzies. Make name-marks on paper for Fuzzies, Fuzzies make finger-marks."

"Why make finga'p'int?" Little Fuzzy asked. "Get idee-disko?" He fingered the silver disc at his throat.

"No; just make finga'p'int. Then, somebody ask Fuzzies, Fuzzies say, yes, saw Big Ones make name-marks."

"But why?" Diamond wanted to know. "Big Ones give Fuzzies nice things now."

"This is playtime for Big Ones," Flora said. "Pappy Ben make play like this all the time, make name-mark on paper."

"That's right," Brannhard said. "This is how Big Ones make play. Much fun; Big Ones call it Law. Now, you watch what Unka Gus do."

vii.

Gus Brannhard said, "Well, I was wrong. I am most happy to admit it. I've been getting the same reports, from all over, and the editorial opinion is uniformly favorable."

Leslie Coombes, in the screen, nodded. He was in the library of his apartment across the city, with a coffee service and a stack of papers and teleprint sheets on the table in front of him.

"Editorial opinion, of course, doesn't win elections, but the grass-roots-level reports are just as good. Things are going to be just as they always were, and that's what most people really want. It ought to gain us some votes, instead of losing us any. These people Hugo Ingermann was frightening with stories about how they were going to be taxed into poverty to maintain the Fuzzies in luxury, for instance. . . . Now it appears that the Fuzzies will be financing the Government."

"Is Victor still in town?"

"Oh, no. He left for Yellowsand Canyon before daybreak. He's been having men and equipment shifted in there from Big Blackwater for the last week. By this time, they're probably digging out sunstones by the peck."

He laughed. Like a kid with a new rifle; couldn't wait to try it out. "I suppose he took Diamond along?"

Grego never went anywhere without his Fuzzy. "Well, why don't you drop around to Government House for cocktails? Jack's still in town, and we can talk without as many interruptions, human and otherwise, as last evening."

Coombes said he would be glad to. They chatted for a few minutes, then broke the connection, and immediately the screen buzzer began. When he put it on again, his screen-girl looked out of it as though she smelled a week-old dead snake somewhere.

"The Honorable—technically, of course—Hugo Ingermann," she said. "He's been trying to get you for the last ten minutes."

"Well, I've been trying to get him ever since I took office," he said. "Put him on." Then he snapped on the recorder.

The screen flickered and cleared, and a plump, well-barbered face looked out of it, affable and candid, with innocently wide blue eyes. A face anybody who didn't know its owner would trust.

"Good morning, Mr. Brannhard."

"Good morning indeed, Mr. Ingermann. Is there something I can do for you? Besides dropping dead, that is?"

"Ah, I believe there is something I can do for you, Mr. Brannhard," Ingermann beamed like an orphanage superintendent on Christmas morning. "How would you like pleas of guilty from Leo Thaxter, Conrad and Rose Evins, and Phil Novaes?"

"I couldn't even consider them. You know pleas of guilty to capital charges aren't admissible."

Ingermann stared for a moment in feigned surprise, then laughed. "Those ridiculous things? No, we are pleading guilty to the proper and legitimate charges of first-degree burglary, grand larceny, and criminal conspiracy. That is, of course, if the Colony agrees to drop that silly farrago of faginy and enslavement charges."

He checked the impulse to ask Ingermann if he were

crazy. Whatever Hugo Ingermann was, he wasn't that. He substituted: "Do you think I'm crazy, Mr. Ingermann?"

"I hope you're smart enough to see the advantage of my offer," Ingermann replied.

"Well, I'm sorry, but I'm not. The advantage to your clients, yes; that's the difference between twenty years in the penitentiary and a ten-millimeter bullet in the back of the head. I'm afraid the advantage to the Colony is slightly less apparent."

"It shouldn't be. You can't get a conviction on those charges, and you know it. I'm giving you a chance to get off the hook."

"Well, that's very kind of you, Mr. Ingermann, indeed it is. I'm afraid, though, that I can't take advantage of your good nature. You'll just have to fight those charges in court."

"You think I can't?" Ingermann was openly contemptuous now. "You're prosecuting my clients, if that's how you mispronounce it, on charges of faginy. You know perfectly well that the crime of faginy cannot be committed against an adult, and you know, just as well, that that's what those Fuzzies are."

"They are legally minor children."

"They are classified as minor children by a court ruling. That ruling is not only contrary to physical fact but is also a flagrant usurpation of legislative power by the judiciary, and hence unconstitutional. As such, I mean to attack it."

And wouldn't that play Nifflheim? The Government couldn't let that ruling be questioned; why, it would . . . Which was what Ingermann was counting on, of course. He shrugged.

"We can get along without convicting them of faginy; we can still convict them of enslavement. That's the nice thing about capital punishment: nobody needs to be shot in the head more than once."

Ingermann laughed scornfully. "You think you can

frame my clients on enslavement charges? Those Fuzzies weren't slaves; they were accomplices."

"They were made drunk, transported under the influence of liquor from their native habitat, confined under restraint, compelled to perform work, and punished for failure to do so by imprisonment in a dungeon, by starvation, and by electric-shock tortures. If that isn't a classic description of the conditions of enslavement, I should like to hear one."

"And have the Fuzzies accused my clients of these crimes?" Ingermann asked. "Under veridication, on a veridicator tested to distinguish between true and false statements when made by Fuzzies?"

No, they hadn't; and that was only half of it. The other half was what he'd been afraid of all along.

"Don't tell me; I'll tell you," Ingermann went on. "They have not, for the excellent reason that Fuzzies can't be veridicated. I have that on the authority of Dr. Ernst Mallin, Victor Grego's chief Fuzzyologist. A polyencephalographic veridicator simply will not respond to Fuzzies. Now, you put those Fuzzies on the stand against my clients and watch what happens."

That was true. Mallin, who had the idea that scientific information ought to be published, had stated that no Fuzzy with whom he had worked had ever changed the blue light of a veridicator to the red of falsehood. He had also stated that in his experience no Fuzzy had ever made a false statement, under veridication or otherwise. But Ingermann was ignoring that.

"And as to these faginy charges, if you people really believe that Fuzzies are legally minor children, why was it thought necessary to have a dozen and a half of them fingerprint that Yellowsand lease agreement? Minor children do not sign documents like that."

He laughed. "Oh, that was just fun for the Fuzzies," he said. "They wanted to do what the Big Ones were doing."

"Mr. Brannhard!" From Ingermann's tone, he might

have been a parent who has just been informed by a five-year-old that a gang of bandits in black masks had come in and looted the cookie jar. "Do you expect me to believe that?"

"I don't give a hoot on Nifflheim whether you do or not, Mr. Ingermann. Now, was there anything else you wanted to talk to me about?"

"Isn't that enough for now?" Ingermann asked. "The trial won't be for a month yet. If, in the meantime, you change your mind—and if you're well-advised you will—just give me a call. Good-bye for now."

Victor Grego's aircar pilot wasn't usually insane . . . only when he got his hands on the controls of a vehicle. Yellowsand Canyon was three time zones east of Mallorysport, and, coming in, the sun was an hour higher than when they had lifted out. Diamond had noticed that too, and commented on it.

A sergeant of the Marine guard met them on the top landing stage of Government House. "Mr. Grego. Mr. Coombes and Mr. Brannhard are here, with the Governor in his office."

"Is anybody here going to try to arrest my Fuzzy?" he asked.

The sergeant grinned. "No, sir. He's been accused of everything but space-piracy, high treason, and murder-one, along with the others, but Marshal Fane says he won't arrest any of them if they show up tomorrow in Complaint Court."

"Thank you, Sergeant. Then, I won't need this." Victor unbuckled his pistol, wrapping the belt around the holster, and tossed it onto the back seat of the car, lifting Diamond and setting him on his shoulder. "Go amuse yourself for a couple of hours," he told the pilot. "Stay around where I can reach you, though."

At the head of the escalator, he told Diamond the same thing, watching him ride down and scamper across the garden in search of Flora and Fauna and the rest of his friends. Then Victor went inside, and found Leslie Coombes and Gus Brannhard seated with Ben Rainsford at the oval table in the private conference room. They exchanged greetings, and he sat down with them.

"Now, what the devil's all this about arresting Fuzzies?" he demanded. "What are they charged with?"

"They aren't charged with anything, yet," Brannhard told him. "Hugo Ingermann made information against all six of them with the Colonial Marshal. He accused Allan Pinkerton and Arsene Lupin and Sherlock Holmes and Irene Adler and Mata Hari of first-degree burglary, grand larceny and criminal conspiracy, and Diamond with misprision of felony and accessory-before-the-fact. They won't be charged till the accusations are heard in Complaint Court tomorrow."

Complaint Court was something like the ancient grand jury—an inquiry into whether or not a chargeable crime had been committed. The accusation was on trial there, not the accused.

"Well, you aren't letting it get past there, are you?"

Before Brannhard could answer, Jack Holloway and Ernst Mallin came in. Holloway was angry, the tips of his mustache twitching and a feral glare in his eyes. He must have looked like that when he beat up Kellogg and shot Borch. Ernst Mallin looked distressed; he'd been in one criminal case involving Fuzzies, and that had been enough. Ahmed Khadra entered behind them, with Fitz Mortlake, the Company Police captain who was guardian-of-record for the other five Fuzzies. After more greetings, they all sat down.

"What are you going to do about this goddamned thing?" Jack Holloway began while he was still pulling up his chair. "You going to let that son of a Khooghra get away with this?"

"If you mean the Fuzzies, hell, no," Brannhard said. "They're not guilty of anything, and everybody, Ingermann included, knows it. He's trying to bluff me into dropping the faginy and enslavement charges and letting his clients cop a plea on the burglary and larceny charges. He thinks I'm afraid to prosecute those faginy and enslavement charges. He's right; I am. But I'm going ahead with them.''

"Well, but, my God . . . !" Jack Holloway began to explode.

"What's wrong with those charges?"

"Well, the faginy, now," Brannhard said. "That's based on the assumption that Fuzzies are equivalent to human children of ten-to-twelve, and that rests on a reversible judicial opinion, not on statute law. Ingermann thinks we'll drop the charges rather than open the Fuzzies' minor-child status to question, because that's the basis of the whole Government Fuzzy policy.''

"And you're afraid of that?"

"Of course he is," Coombes said. "So am I, and so ought you to be. Just take the Yellowsand agreement. If the Fuzzies are legally minor children, they can't control or dispose of property. The Government, as guardian-in-general of the whole Fuzzy race, has authority to do that, including leasing mineral lands. But suppose they're adult aborigines. Even Class-IV aborigines can control their own property, and according to Federation Law, Terrans are forbidden to settle upon or exploit the 'anciently accustomed habitation' of Class-IV natives— in this case, Beta Continent north of the Snake and the Little Blackwater, which includes Yellowsand Canyon —without the natives' consent. Consent, under Federation Law, must be expressed by vote of a representative tribal council, or by the will of a recognized tribal chief.''

"Well, Jesus-in-the-haymow!" Jack Holloway almost yelled. "There is no such damned thing! They have no tribes, just little family groups, about half a dozen in each. And who in Nifflheim ever heard of a Fuzzy chief?''

"Then, we're all right," he said. "The law cannot compel the performance of an impossibility.''

"You only have half of that, Victor," Coombes said. "The law, for instance, cannot compel a blind man to pass a vision test. The law, however, can and does make passing such a test a requirement for operating a contragravity vehicle. Blind men cannot legally pilot aircars. So if we can't secure the consent of a nonexistent Fuzzy tribal council, we can't mine sunstones at Yellowsand, lease or no lease."

"Then, we'll get out all we can while the lease is still good." He'd stripped Big Blackwater of men and equipment already; he was thinking of what other Peters could be robbed to pay Yellowsand Paul. "We have a month till the trial."

"I'm just as interested in that as you are, Victor," Gus Brannhard said, "but that's not the only thing. There's the Adoption Bureau: If the Fuzzies aren't minor children, somebody might make enslavement—peonage at least—out of those adoptions. And the health and education programs. And the hokfusine—sooner or later some damned do-gooder'll squawk about compulsory medication. And here's another angle: Under Colonial Law, nobody is chargeable with any degree of homicide in any case of a person killed while committing a felony. As minor children of under twelve, Fuzzies are legally incapable of committing felony. But if they're legally adults . . ."

Jack literally howled. "Then, anybody could shoot a Fuzzy, anytime, if he caught him breaking into something, or . . ."

"Well, say we drop the faginy charges," Fitz Mortlake suggested. "We still have the other barrel loaded. They can be shot just as dead for enslavement as for enslavement and faginy."

"Is the other barrel loaded, though?" Gus asked. "I can put that gang on the stand—thank all the gods and the man who invented the veridicator, there's no law against self-incrimination—I can't force them to talk. You can't do things in open court like you can in the back room at a police station. I may be able to get a conviction without the Fuzzies' testimony, but I can't guarantee it. Tell him about it, Dr. Mallin.''

"Well." Ernst Mallin cleared his throat. "Well," he said again. "You all understand the principles of the polyencephalographic veridicator. All mental activity is accompanied by electromagnetic activity, in detectable wave patterns. The veridicator is so adjusted as to respond only to the wave patterns accompanying the suppression of a true statement and the substitution of a false statement, by causing the blue light in the globe to turn red. I have used the veridicator in connection with psychological experiments with quite a few Fuzzies. I have never had one change the blue light to red.''

He didn't go into the legal aspects of that; that wasn't his subject. It was Gus Brannhard's:

"And court testimony, no exception, must be given under veridication, with a veridicator tested by having a test-witness make a random series of true and false statements. If Fuzzies can't be veridicated, then Fuzzies can't testify—like Leslie's blind man flying an aircar.''

"Yes, and that'll play Nifflheim, too," Ahmed Khadra said. "How do you think we'll prosecute anybody for mistreating Fuzzies if the Fuzzies can't testify against him?''

"Or somebody claims Fuzzy adoptions are enslavement," Ben Rainsford said. "Victor's Diamond, for instance, or my Flora and Fauna. How could we prove that our Fuzzies are happy with us and wouldn't want to live anywhere else, if they can't testify to it?''

"Wait a minute. I'm just a layman," Grego said, "but I know that every accused person is entitled to testify in his own defense. These Fuzzies are accused persons, thanks to Hugo Ingermann himself.''

Brannhard laughed. "Ingermann's hoping to hang us on that," he said. "He expects Leslie, who's defending them, to put them on the stand in Complaint Court, so that I'll have to attack their eligibility to testify and stop myself from using their testimony against his clients. Well, we won't do it that way. Leslie'll just plead them not guilty but chargeable and waive hearing.''

"But then they'll all have to stand trial," Grego objected.

"Sure they will." The Attorney General's laugh became a belly-shaking guffaw. "Remember the last time a bunch of Fuzzies got loose in court? We'll just let them act like Fuzzies, and see what it does to Ingermann's claim that they're mature and responsible adults.''

"Dr. Mallin," Coombes said suddenly. "You say you never saw a Fuzzy red-light a veridicator. Did you ever hear a Fuzzy make a demonstrably false statement under veridication?''

"To my knowledge, I never heard a Fuzzy make a demonstrably false statement under any circumstances, Mr. Coombes.''

"Ah. And in *People* versus *Kellogg and Holloway* you gave testimony about extensive studies you had made of Fuzzies' electroencephalographic patterns. So their mental activity is accompanied by electromagnetic activity?''

Maybe it might be a good thing to have a lawyer sit in on every scientific discussion, just to see that the rules of evidence are applied. Mallin gave one of his tight little smiles.

"Precisely, Mr. Coombes. Fuzzies exhibit the same general wave-patterns as Terrans or any other known sapient race. All but the suppression-substitution pattern which triggers the light-change in the veridicator. No detection instrument can function in the absence of the event it is intended to detect. Fuzzies simply do not suppress true statements and substitute false statements. That is, they do not lie.''

"That'll be one hell of a thing to try to prove," Gus Brannhard said. "Fitz, you questioned those Fuzzies under veridication after the gem-vault job, didn't you?''

"Yes. Ahmed and Miss Glenn interpreted for them; Diamond helped too. The veridicator had been tested; we used scaled down electrodes and a helmet made up in the robo-service shop at Company House. We got nothing but blue from any of them. We accepted that."

"I would have, too," Brannhard said. "But in court we'll have to show that the veridicator would have redlighted if any of them had tried to lie."

"We need Fuzzy test-witnesses, to lie under veridication," Coombes said. "If they don't know how to lie, we'll have to teach a few. I believe that will be Dr. Mallin's job; I will help. Do any of you gentlemen collect paradoxes? This one's a gem—to prove that Fuzzies tell the truth, we must first prove that they tell lies. You know, that's one of the things I love about the law."

Everybody laughed, except Jack Holloway. He sat staring glumly at the tabletop.

"So now, along with everything else we've got to make liars out of them too," he said. "I wonder what we'll finally end up making them."

viii.

Ahead, the ravine fell sharply downward; on either side it rose high and steep above the little moving-water. The trees were not many here, but there were large rocks. They had to dodge among and climb over them, going in single file. Sometimes he led, and sometimes they would all be ahead of him, Fruitfinder and Lame One and Big She and Other She and Stabber and Carries-Bright-Things and Stonebreaker. They were not hunting —there was nothing to eat here—but ahead he could see blue sky above the trees and could hear the sound of another moving-water which this one joined.

Wise One hoped it would not be too deep or too rapid to cross. There was much moving-water here in all the low places between the hills and mountains. A place of much water was good because they could always drink when thirsty and because the growing-things they ate and the animals they hunted were more near water. But moving-waters were often hard to cross, and if they followed one they would come to where it joined another, and it would be big too. Without seeing it, he knew that this one flowed in the direction of the sun's left hand, for that was how the land sloped. Moving-waters always went down, never up, and they joined bigger ones. That was an always-so thing.

Then, before they knew it, they were out of the ravine

and the woods stretched away on either side and in front
of them and the moving-water was small and easy to
cross. On the other side, the ground sloped up gently
away from it, then rose in a steep mountainside. This
would be a good place to find things to eat. They
splashed across at a shallow place and ran up the bank,
laughing and shouting, and spread out line-abreast,
hunting under the big trees toward the side of the mountain. There were brown-nut trees here. They picked up
sticks and stones and threw them to knock nuts down,
and then Big She shouted:

"Look, nuts here already fall off tree. Many-many on
ground."

It was so; the ground at the bottom of one tree was
covered with them. They all ran quickly, gathering
under the tree, laying nuts on big stones and pounding
them with little ones to break the shells to get at the
white inside. They were good, and enough for everybody; they ate as fast as they could crack them. They
were all careful, though, to watch and listen, for in a
place like this there was always danger. Animals could
not hear their voices—that was an always-so thing which
they could trust—but they made much noise cracking
the nuts, and animals which hunted People would hear
it and know what it was.

So they kept their clubs to hand, so that they could
catch them up if they had to run quickly, and Carries-
Bright-Things kept the three sticks with the bright-
things on the ends with her club. They would not be able
to stay here long, he thought. Long enough to eat as
many of the nuts as they wanted, but no longer. He
began to think whether to go down the stream or climb
up the side of the mountain. Along the stream they
would find more good-to-eat things, but the sun was
well past highest-time, and they might find a better
sleeping-place on the mountaintop. But this moving-
water went in the direction of the sun's left hand, and
that was the way he wanted to go.

They had been traveling steadily toward the sun's left hand for many days now. It was an always-so thing that after leaf-turning time, when the leaves became brown and fell, it became more cold toward the sun's right hand and stayed warmer to the sun's left; and People liked being where it was warm. Far to the sun's right hand, farther than he had ever been, it was said that it grew so cold at times that little pools of still water would be edged with hardness from the cold. This he had never seen for himself, but other People had told about it. So, ever since the day when they had seen the gotza killed by the thunder-death and had found the bright-things, they had been moving toward the sun's left hand.

He himself had another, even stronger, reason. Ever since he had seen the two Big Ones inside the flying thing, he had been determined to find the Big One Place.

He did not speak about this to the others. They were content to go where Wise One led them; but if he told them what was in his mind, they would all cry out against it and there would be argument, and nothing would be done. The others were still afraid of the flying Big Ones, especially Big She and Fruitfinder and Stonebreaker. He could understand that. It was always well to be at least a little afraid of something one did not know about, and a strange kind of People who went about in flying things and made thunder-death that killed gotza in the air could be very dangerous. But he was sure that they would be friendly.

They had killed the three gotza that had threatened him and the others at the cliff where they had been eating the hatta-zosa; they had been watching from above, and had done nothing until the gotza came, and then they had turned loose the thunder-death, and then they had gone away, leaving the three bright-things. And after chasing the other gotza in their flying thing and killing it, they had passed directly over him and the others, and must have seen them, but they had done no harm. That had been when he had made up his mind to find the Big One Place, and make friends with them. But when he had spoken of it to the others, they had all been afraid. All but Stabber; he had wanted to make friends with the Big Ones too, but when the others had been afraid he had said no more about it.

That had been two hands of sun-times and dark-times ago. Since then, they had seen flying things four times, always to the sun's left hand. He knew nothing about the country in that direction, but to the sun's right hand nobody had ever told of seeing flying things. So, he was sure, in order to find the Big One Place, he must go toward the sun's left hand. But he must not speak about it to the others, only say that it would be warmer to the sun's left hand, and talk about how they might find many zatku.

There was a crashing in the brush in the direction the moving-water came from, as though some big animal was running very fast. If so, something bigger was chasing it. He sprang to his feet, his club in one hand and the stone with which he had been cracking nuts in the other. The others were on their feet, ready to flee too, when a takku came rushing straight toward them.

Takku were not dangerous; they ate only growing-things. People did not hunt them, however, because they were big and too fleet of foot to catch. But behind the takku something else was coming, making more noise, and it would be something dangerous. He hurled his stone, throwing a little ahead of the takku, meaning to drive it and whatever was after it away from them. To his surprise, he hit it on the flank.

"Throw stones!" he shouted. "Chase takku away!"

The others understood; they snatched up stones and pelted the takku. One stone hit it on the neck. It swerved away from them, stumbled, and was trying to regain its feet when the hesh-nazza burst from the brush behind it and caught it.

Hesh-nazza were the biggest animals in the woods.

They had three horns, one jutting from the middle of the forehead and one curving back from each lower jaw. Except for the gotza, which attacked from above, no animal was more feared by the People, and even the gotza never attacked a hesh-nazza. Catching up with the takku, the hesh-nazza gored it in the side, in back of the shoulder, with its forehead-horn. The takku bleated in pain, and continued to bleat while the hesh-nazza struck it with its forefeet and freed its horn to gore again.

The Gashta did not stay to see what happened after that. The takku was still bleating as they ran up the mountainside; as they climbed, it stopped, and then the hesh-nazza gave a great bellow, as they always did after killing. By this time it would be tearing the flesh of the takku with its jaw-horns, and eating. He was glad he had thought to throw the stone, and tell the others to throw; if he had not, the takku would have run straight among them, and the hesh-nazza after it, and that would have been bad. Now, however, there was no danger, but they continued climbing until they were at the top. Then they all stopped, breathing hard, to rest.

"Better hesh-nazza eat takku than us," Lame One said.

"Big takku," Stabber remarked. "Hesh-nazza eat long time. Then go to sleep. Next sun-time, be hungry, hunt again."

"Hesh-nazza not come up here," Carries-Bright-Things said. "Stay by moving-water, in low place."

She was right; hesh-nazza did not like to climb steep places. They stayed by moving-waters, and hunted by lying quietly and waiting for animals, or for People, to come by. He was glad that he and the others had not crossed farther up the stream.

It would still be daylight for a time, but the sun was low enough that they should begin to think about finding a good sleeping-place. The top of this mountain was big and he could see nothing ahead but woods—big trees, some nut-trees. This would be a good place to sleep, and after the sun came out of its sleeping-place, they could go down into the low place on the other side.

"Go down way we came up," Big She argued. Lately, Big She was beginning to be contrary. "Good place; nut-trees."

"Bad place; hesh-nazza," Stabber told her. "Hesh-nazza go down moving-water little way, wait. We come, then we be inside hesh-nazza. Better do what Wise One say; Wise One knows best."

"First, find sleeping-place here," he said. "Now we go hunt. Everybody, look for good place to sleep."

The others agreed. They had seen nut-trees here too; where there were nut-trees, there were small animals, good to eat, which gnawed nut-shells open. They might kill and eat a few. Nuts were good, but meat was better. There might even be zatku up here.

They spread out, calling back and forth to one another, being careful to make no noise with their feet among the dead leaves. He thought about the takku. He and at least one of the others had hit it with stones. A person could throw a stone hard enough to knock down and sometimes even kill a hatta-zosa, but all the stones had done to the takku had been to frighten it. He wished there were some way People could kill takku. One takku would be meat enough for everybody all day, and some to carry to the sleeping-place for the next morning; and from a takku's leg-bones good clubs could be made.

He wished he knew how the Big Ones made the thunder-death. Anything that killed a gotza in the air would kill a takku. Why, anything that would kill a gotza would even kill a hesh-nazza! There must be no animal of which the Big Ones were afraid.

It had been a week before Jack Holloway had been able to get away from Mallorysport and back to Hoksu-Mitto, and by that time the new permanent office building was finished and furnished. He had a nice big room on the first floor, complete, of course, with a stack of paperwork that had accumulated on his desk in his absence. The old prefab hut had been taken down and moved across the run, and set up beside the schoolhouse as additional living quarters for Fuzzies, of whom there were now four hundred. That was a hell of a lot of Fuzzies.

"They're costing like hell too," George Lunt said. George and Gerd van Riebeek, who had returned from Yellowsand Canyon the day after the lease agreement had been signed, and Pancho Ybarra were with him in his new office the morning after his return. "And we have a hundred to a hundred and fifty more at the outposts, and hokfusine and Extee Three to supply to the families living on farms and plantations."

George didn't need to tell him that. A lot of what had piled up on his desk had to do with supplies bought or on order. And the Native Commission payroll: two hundred fifty ZNPF officers and men, Ahmed Khadra's investigators, the technicians and construction men, the clerical force, the men and women working under Gerd van Riebeek in the scientific bureau, Lynne Andrews and her medical staff. . . .

"If that Yellowsand agreement goes out the airlock," Gerd van Riebeek voiced his own thoughts, "we'll have a hell of a lot of bills to pay and nothing to pay them with."

Nobody argued that point. Pancho Ybarra said, "It's on the Fuzzy Reservation; doesn't the Colonial Government control that?"

"Not the way we need, not if the Fuzzies aren't minor children. The Government controls the Reservation to enforce the law; that means, if the Fuzzies are legally adults, nobody is permitted to mine sunstones on the Reservation without the Fuzzies' consent."

"Those fingerprint signatures on that agreement," George Lunt considered. "I know, they were only additional witnesses, but weren't they acquiescent witnesses?

Wouldn't that do as evidence of consent?''

Gus Brannhard had thought of that a couple of days ago. Maybe that would stand up in court; Chief Justice Pendarvis had declined to give a guidance-opinion on it, which didn't look too good.

"Well, then, let's get their consent," Gerd said. "We have over four hundred here; that's the most Fuzzies in any one place on the planet. Let's hold a Fuzzy election. Elect Little Fuzzy paramount chief, and elect about a dozen subchiefs, and hold a tribal council, and vote consent to lease Yellowsand to the Company. You ought to see some of the tribal councils on Yggdrasil; at least ours would be sober.''

"Or Gimli; I was stationed there before I was transferred to Zarathustra," Lunt said. "That's how the Gimli Company got consent to work those fissionable-ore mines.''

"Won't do. According to law, what one of these tribal councils has to do is vote somebody something like a power of attorney to transact their business for them, and that has to be veridicated by the native chief or council or whatever granting it," he said.

Silence fell with a dull thump. The four of them looked at one another. Lunt said:

"With that much money involved, a couple of lawyers like Gus Brannhard and Leslie Coombes ought to be able to find some way around the law.''

"I don't want to have to get around the law," Holloway said. "If we get around the law to help the Fuzzies, somebody else'll take the same road around it to hurt them." His pipe had gone out, and there was nothing in it but ashes when he tried to relight it. He knocked it into an ashtray and got out his tobacco pouch. "This isn't just for this week or this year. There'll be Fuzzies and other people living together on this planet for thousands of years, and we want to start Fuzzy-Human relations off right. We don't know who'll run the Government and the Company after Rainsford and Grego and the rest of us are dead. They will run things on precedents we establish now."

He was talking more to himself than to the three men in the office with him. He puffed on the pipe, and then continued.

"That's why I want to see Leo Thaxter and Evins and his wife and Phil Novaes shot for what they did to those Fuzzies. I'm not bloodthirsty; I've killed enough people myself that I don't see any fun in it. I just want the law clear and plain that Fuzzies are entitled to the same protection as human children, and I want a precedent to warn anybody else of what they'll get if they mistreat Fuzzies."

"I agree," Pancho Ybarra said. "In my professional opinion, to which I will testify, that's exactly what Fuzzies are—innocent and trusting little children, as helpless and vulnerable in human society as human children are in adult society. And the gang who enslaved and tortured those Fuzzies to make thieves out of them ought to be shot, not so much for what they did as for being the sort of people who would do it."

"What do you think about the veridication angle?" Lunt asked. "If we can't get that cleared up, we won't be able to do anything."

"Well, if a Fuzzy doesn't red-light a veridicator, it means the Fuzzy isn't lying," Gerd said. "You ever know a Fuzzy to lie? I've never known one to; neither has Ruth."

"Neither have I, not even the ones we've caught raising hell down in the farming country," Lunt said. "Every man on the Protection Force'll testify to that."

"Well, what's Mallin doing?" Gerd asked. "Is he going to get Henry Stenson to invent an instrument that'll detect a Fuzzy telling the truth?"

"No. He's going to teach some Fuzzies to lie so they can red-light a veridicator and show that it works."

"Hey, he can get shot for that!" Lunt said. "Lying is an immoral act. That's faginy!"

• • •

One of the Fuzzies, whose name was Kraft, sat cross-legged on the floor, smoking a pipe. The other was named Ebbing; she sat in a scaled-down veridicator chair, with a chromium helmet on her head. Behind her, a translucent globe mounted on a standard glowed clear blue. Ernst Mallin sat sidewise at the table, looking at them; across from him, Leslie Coombes was smoking a cigarette in silence.

"Ebbing, you want to help Unka Ernst, Unka Less'ee?" he was asking for the *n*th time.

"Sure," Ebbing agreed equably. "What want Ebbing do?"

"Your name Ebbing. You understand name?"

"Sure. Name something somebody call somebody else. Big Ones give all Fuzzies names; put names on idee-disko." She fingered the silver disk at her throat. "My name here. Ebbing."

"She knows that?" Coombes asked.

"Oh, yes. She can even print it for you, as neatly as it's engraved on the disk. Now, Ebbing. Unka Less'ee ask what your name, you tell him name is Kraft."

"But is not. My name Ebbing. Kraft *his* name." She pointed.

"I know. Unka Less'ee know too. But Unka Less'ee ask, you say Kraft. Then he ask Kraft, Kraft say his name Ebbing."

"Is Big One way to make fun," Coombes interjected. "We call it, Alias, Alias, Who's Got the Alias. Much fun."

"Please, Mr. Coombes. Now, Ebbing, you say to Unka Less'ee your name is Kraft."

"You mean, make trade with Kraft? Trade idee-disko too?"

"No. Real name for you Ebbing. You just *say* name is Kraft."

The blue-lit globe flickered, the color in it swirling, changing to dark indigo and back to pale blue. For a moment he was hopeful, then realized that it was only the typical confusion-of-meaning effect. Ebbing touched her ID-disk and looked at her companion. Then the light settled to clear blue.

"Kraft," she said calmly.

"Unholy Saint Beelzebub!" Coombes groaned.

He felt like groaning himself.

"You give new idee-disko?" Ebbing asked.

"She thinks her name is Kraft now. That's telling the truth to the best of her knowledge and belief," Coombes said.

"No, no; name for you Ebbing; name for him Kraft." He rose and went to her, detaching the helmet and electrodes. "Finish for now," he said. "Go make play. Tell Auntie Anne give estee-fee."

The Fuzzies started to dash out, then remembered their manners, stopped at the door to say, "Sank-oo, Unka Ernst; goo-bye, Unka Less'ee, Unka Ernst," before scampering away.

"They both believe now that I meant that they should trade names," he said. "The next time I see them, they'll be wearing each other's ID-disks, I suppose."

"They don't even know that lying is possible," Coombes said. "They don't have anything to lie about naturally. Their problems are all environmental, and you can't lie to your environment; if you try to lie to yourself about it, it kills you. I wish their social structure was a little more complicated; lying is a social custom. I wish they'd invented politics!"

ix.

Wise One was glad when they came to where the mountain "made finish" and dropped away, far down. This had not been a good place. There had been nut-trees, and they had eaten nuts. They had killed some of the little nut-eating animals, but not many, for they were hard to catch. They had found no moving-water on top of the mountain, only small pools of still-water from the last rain, and it had not tasted good. And the sleeping-place they had found had not been good either, and it had been one of the nights when both of the night-time lights had been in the sky, and the animals had all been restless, and they had heard a screamer, though not near. Screamers ate only meat and hunted in the dark. That had been why they had found no hatta-zosa. Hatta-zosa did not stay where there were screamers. Neither did People, if they could help it.

They stopped, looking out over the tops of the trees to the country beyond. There was another mountain far to the sun's left hand; its top stretched away, from sun-upward to sun-downward, with nothing but the sky beyond it. It was not steep, and its side was wrinkled with small valleys that showed where moving-waters came down. There must be a big moving-water below, so close to the bottom of this mountain that they could not see it. It must be a large one, because of all the little ones on both sides that flowed into it, and he was afraid it would be hard to cross.

The others were excited about the wide valley on the other side, and talked about what good hunting they would find there. They couldn't see the moving-water below, so they didn't think about it.

They started down, and as they went the mountainside grew steeper, and they had to cling to bushes and stop to rest against trees and use their killing-clubs to help them. As they went, they began to see the moving-water below. The sound of it grew louder. Finally they were seeing it all the time, and could see how big it was.

Big She began talking about turning back and climbing up to the top again.

"Moving-water too big; we not can cross," she argued. "Go down, no place to go. Better we go back up now."

"Then go beside it, way it come from," Lame One said. "Find place to cross where it little."

"Not find good-to-eat things," Big She said. "Not find good-to-eat things since last daytime. Why Wise One not find good-to-eat things?"

Stabber became angry. "You think you wise like Wise One?" he demanded. "You think you find good-to-eat things?"

"Hungry," Fruitfinder complained. "Want to find good-to-eat things now. Maybe Big She right. Maybe better go back, go down other side."

"You want, you go back up mountain," he said. "We go down. Cross moving-water, find good-to-eat things other side."

Carries-Bright-Things agreed; so did Lame One and Other She. They started climbing down again; Big She and Stonebreaker and Fruitfinder followed without saying anything. At length the mountain became less steep, and through the trees they saw the moving-water in front of them. They went forward and stopped on the bank.

It was big, wide, and swift. Lame One picked up a stone and threw it as hard as he could; it splashed far short of the other bank. Other She threw a stick into it, and in an instant it was carried away out of sight. Even if they had been willing to risk losing their killing-clubs and the bright-things, they could never have swum across it. Big She pointed at it with her club.

"Look! Look at place Wise One bring us!" she clamored. "No good-to-eat things; no way across river. Now, climb all the way back up mountain."

"Climb up high-steep place?" Other She was horrified.

"You try cross that?" Big She retorted. Then she looked downstream and saw where the river curved away from the mountain. "Maybe go down there."

"That way moving-water we cross last day-time come down," he said. "Hesh-nazza that way. Eat all takku, be hungry, now."

Big She had forgotten about the hesh-nazza, and Big She was afraid of hesh-nazza, more even than the others. Once a hesh-nazza had almost caught her. She went back to insisting that they climb the mountain again. Fruitfinder thought they should, too. Stabber thought they ought to go up the river, which was the only thing to do. Finally all the others, even Big She, agreed.

It was hard going. The river flowed close against the mountain now, there was no bank, and they had to go in single file, clinging to bushes and trees as they went. Big She began complaining again, and so did some of the others.

Then, suddenly, they were around the shoulder of the mountain and there was a wide level place in front where a small valley opened out, with a little stream small enough to cross easily. Here the river was three or four stone-throws wide, and flowed among and over stones, shallow and flashing in the sunlight, and on both sides were long stony beaches, littered with old driftwood.

They started across. Mostly it was less than waist deep. In a few places it was deeper, and they formed a chain, each one holding to somebody else's killing-club. Finally, they were on the beach on the other side, and everybody, even Big She, was happy.

There was much driftwood here, even whole trees. This must be a place where the moving-water was high over the banks in rain-time. They all looked at the drift-wood, and talked about what good killing-clubs it would make. They would have stopped to make new clubs, except that they were all hungry. They decided to hunt for food and then come back after they had eaten. So they started away from the river, into the woods, calling to one another.

There were no nut-trees here, but they found the pink fingerlike growing-things. They were good, but one could eat a great deal of them and still be hungry. But zatku also liked to eat them, and they found where zatku had been nibbling and, hunting carefully, found three. That was more zatku in one day than anybody could remember. And they found other things to eat, animals and growing-things, and by a little after sun-highest time none of them was hungry.

So they made their way back to the beach, and as they went they found where three fallen trees, washed out by the floods, lay together with a little gulley under them. This was a good sleeping-place; they would remember it and come back when the sun began to get low.

They looked again at the driftwood on the beach, dry and hard and white as the bones of animals. Wise One found nothing that would make a better club than the one he carried. It was a good club. He had worked a long time to make it. Some of the others didn't have good clubs, and they found straight branches that could be worked down. Some of the stones on the beach were very hard, and Stonebreaker, who was good at such work, began chipping them, making chopping-stones. Big She and Fruitfinder and Carries-Bright-Things squatted with him, watching him work and talking to him. Other She found a good piece of wood and a flat stone and sat down, holding the stick against one of the old trees and rubbing it with the stone to shape it. Lame One was also making a new club, and so was Stabber, who sat a little apart from the others. Wise One went over and sat with Stabber, who showed him the new club he was making. It was long, for stabbing.

"Good place, this," Stabber said as he worked. "Many good-to-eat things. Find three zatku." He was amazed at that. "More zatku here, many-many. And hatta-zosa. Find where they eat bark on trees." He rubbed the pointed end of his new club, sharpening it. "We stay here?"

"We have sleeping-place; maybe stay next day-time," he said. "Then go, find little moving-water, follow to where comes out of ground. Go up to top of mountain, go down other side."

"Other side like this. Why not stay here?"

"Other side more to sun's left hand. Big One Place to sun's left hand. Find Big Ones, make friends. Big Ones help us. Big Ones very wise, we learn from them," he said. "You want to find Big Ones?"

"I want to find Big Ones," Stabber said. "Others not want, others afraid. Listen to Big She." He laid down the stone and took the club in both hands, inspecting it. "Big She think she knows more than Wise One. Stone-breaker, Fruitfinder listen to her."

That was how bands broke up. It had happened once, long ago, when Old One was still alive and leading the band. There had been quarreling about where to go to hunt, and four of the band had gone away angry. They had never seen them again. Stabber's mother had stayed with the band; Stabber had been born two new-leaf times after that. He didn't want that to happen now. Eight People made a good band: not too many to find food for all, and enough to hunt line-abreast so that one would see what another missed, and enough to make a

good hatta-zosa killing. And he did not want quarreling; it was not fun when People quarreled.

But he was going to the Big One Place, to find the Big
Ones and make friends with them, even if he had to go
alone. No, Stabber would go with him, and he thought
Carries-Bright-Things would, too. And that would be
another trouble-thing. If the band broke up, there would
be quarreling about the bright-things.

Maybe Lame One and Other She would go with him,
too. But who would lead the others? Big She wanted to
lead, but she was not Wise One. She was Foolish One,
Shoumko; if the others let her lead, soon they would all
make dead. He wanted to keep the band together.

The sun went slowly across the sky toward its sleeping-place; the shadows grew longer. Stonebreaker was
still chipping the hard stone, making a knife to use for
cutting up hatta-zosa for the meat-sharing. They would
carry it as long as they could, and the stone hand-
chopper he had made. He wished they could carry more
things with them, but a person had only two hands, and
the killing-club must always be carried. Soon the tools
Stonebreaker was making would be left behind and forgotten, or lost in crossing a moving-water. It was a
wonder they had carried the bright-things as long as
they had.

Lame One and Other She had finished their clubs;
they went up the river along the bank. Stabber finished
the weapon he was making; together they went down the
river, past where the stream they had crossed the day
before came in from the other side. They talked about
the hesh-nazza they had seen the day before, and wondered where it was now. It could not cross, because the
river was too deep and swift, and it was too big to get
around the shoulder of the mountain to the shallow
water where they had crossed.

They circled into the woods away from the river,
coming back. They found no animals, but they each
caught several of the little lizards and ate them. When

they came back to the driftwood place, Lame One and Other She were back too, and had brought a hatta-zosa they had killed. They all ate, and by this time the sun was making colors in the sky, very pretty. They all watched until the colors were gone, and then went to the sleeping-place they had found. Everybody was happy, and they talked for a long time before going to sleep.

The next morning the sun made red colors all over the sky, even before it came out of its sleeping-place. They were prettier than last sundown-time, but everybody knew that it would rain, and nobody liked rain. They went to where Lame One and Other She had killed the hatta-zosa the day before, and killed three more of them. By the time they had eaten the last one, drops of rain were beginning to fall, and the sun had hidden itself and the sky was gray and black. They ran all the way back to the sleeping-place.

For a long time, they huddled together under the fallen trees; they could not keep completely dry, but they were out of the worst of the rain. Their fur was wet and clung to them, but they were not really cold, and they had eaten plenty of meat, which made them feel good.

Finally, the rain stopped. The things in the woods began to stir again, and after a while there were thin gleams of sunlight. Everybody was glad. They crawled out and talked about what they would do, and decided to go away from the river, toward the high ground, where they had not been before, and see what was there. Because they might find a better sleeping-place, they carried with them the knife and chopper Stonebreaker had made, and the bright-things.

They went to sun-upward, bearing up the slope toward the sun's left hand. They found many of the pink finger-things growing in shady places, and ate them. Zatku had been eating there, too; they hunted in tight circles, and soon found one, and then another. By this time they were all praising Wise One for bringing them to this good place, even Big She.

"Better than to sun's right hand," he told them. "More warm; this is everybody-know thing. We go to top of mountain, down other side. Everything better there."

Big She tried to argue; this was a good place; why go someplace else? Fruitfinder agreed with her. The others all said, "Wise One know best."

"How you know, better across mountain?" Big She challenged.

"Because is so. Is everybody-know thing." He tried to think how he knew, but couldn't. He knew why he wanted to go toward the sun's left hand, but he couldn't explain about finding the Big One Place without starting more quarreling. "Long-ago People tell," he said. That was something they would not argue about. "Long-ago People hear from other People," he went on, improvising. "Far-far to sun's left hand is good place. Always warm. Always find good-to-eat things. Many zatku, many hatta-zosa, all kinds of good-to-eat growing-things. Everything all the time, not something one time, something another time. Groundberries, redberries, tree-nuts, all good things all the time."

He didn't know there was anything like that to the sun's left hand at all; he was just making talk that it was so. But he was Wise One; the others thought that he knew.

"You listen to Wise One," Stabber said. "Wise One take us to good place."

"I not hear talk like that," Big She objected.

"You not remember," Stabber jeered. "You not remember hesh-nazza day before."

"My mother make talk like that." He wondered if maybe she hadn't, and wished he could remember more about her. A gotza had killed her when he had been very small. "Old One make talk, say she heard from other People." He turned to Carries-Bright-Things. "Old One your mother; she tell you."

Carries-Bright-Things looked puzzled. He knew she couldn't remember anything like that, but she thought she ought to. Finally, she nodded.

"Yes. Old One tell me," she said.

"Everybody-know thing," Lame One said. "All long-ago People tell about good place to sun's left hand."

Other She fidgeted. She couldn't remember anything like that at all, but all the others said they did. Maybe she had forgotten. They started off again, and found another zatku.

But Wise One hadn't heard any such long-ago People stories. He had just made talk that he had. He couldn't understand how he had been able to make not-so talk like that.

x.

It was election day at Hoksu-Mitto. Not Fuzzy tribal election; this was for Big Ones, for delegates to the Constitutional Convention, and it had been going on all over the planet, starting hours ago at Kellytown on Epsilon Continent.

Voting was a simple matter. Jack Holloway had exercised his right of suffrage in his own living room after finishing breakfast by screening the Constabulary post two hundred odd miles south of him and transmitting his fingerprints there. Then he loaded his pipe, and before he had it drawing properly the robot at Constabulary Fifteen had sent his prints to Red Hill. The election robot there had transmitted them to the planetary election office in Central Courts Building in Mallorysport on Alpha Continent, then reported back that Jack Holloway, of Hoksu-Mitto, formerly Holloway's Camp, was a properly registered voter, and the machine gave a small cluck and ejected a photoprinted ballot. He marked the ballot with an X after the name of the Hon. Horace Stannery, an undistinguished and rather less-than-brilliant lawyer in Red Hill but a loyal Company and Government man, and held it up to the transmitting screen.

The whole thing was handled precisely and secretly by incorruptible robots. At least, that was what all the school civics books said. He carried the ballot original over and put it in the drawer of his big table. Hang onto that, he thought; be a museum-piece in half a century. Then he put on the telecast screen while he drank another cup of coffee.

The Gamma Continent vote was all in, what there was of it. Ten seats on the Convention, eight of them Government-CZC regulars. In his own district on Beta, seventy-eight votes, his own included, had given Stannery sixty-two, with the remaining sixteen divided between the two wildcat candidates. It was rather like that all over the continent. Alpha, where a hundred ten out of a hundred fifty seats were being contested, hadn't begun to vote yet; it was only 0445 there.

He kept a telecast screen on in his office throughout the morning. By noon, nine out of ten of the Rainsford-Grego slate were well in the lead everywhere. The polls had closed on Epsilon Continent: eighteen out of eighteen regulars elected. It went on like that all afternoon, and by cocktail time the election looked safe. They'd really have something to drink a toast to this afternoon.

The Fuzzies didn't seem to know that anything out of the ordinary was happening.

Gerd van Riebeek was bothered. Not seriously worried, just nagged by a few small uncertainties and doubts. In the last three weeks, the Protection Force patrol, working to a radius of five hundred miles from Hoksu-Mitto, hadn't reported seeing a single harpy. In that time, there had been two shot in the Fuzzy country south of the Divide, and another one in the Yellowsand Valley to the north. But not one anywhere near Hoksu-Mitto in the last week. It was looking like Zarathustran pseudopterodactyls were becoming about as extinct as the Terran variety.

There hadn't been many to start with, of course.

Their kills would have wiped out everything else long ago if there had been. Say, one harpy to about a hundred or two hundred square miles. And once *Homo s. terra* moved into the area, those wouldn't last long. People liked to be able to let the children run around outdoors, for one thing, and nobody wanted all the calves in a veldbeest herd eaten up before they could grow up. The harpy might have been lord of the Zarathustran skies before the Terrans came, but what chance had it against an aircar rated at Mach 3, carrying a couple of machine guns?

Not that Gerd liked harpies any better than anybody else; not even that he liked them, period. Along with everybody else on Zarathustra, he was convinced that there were two kinds of harpies—live ones and good ones. But he was a general naturalist; ecology was a big part of his subject, and he knew that as soon as you wipe out any single species, things that will affect a dozen other species are going to start happening because every living thing has a role in the general ecological drama.

Harpies were killers. All right, they kept something down; remove them, and that something would have a sudden increase, and that would deplete something they fed on. Or they would begin competing with some other species. And there could be side effects. There was that old story about how the cats killed the field mice and the field mice destroyed the bumblebees' nests. But the bumblebees pollenated clover; so, when the bird-lovers started shooting cats—just the way the Fuzzy-lovers were shooting harpies—the clover crop started to fail. Wasn't that something Darwin wrote up, back about the beginning of the first century Pre-Atomic?

The trouble was, he wasn't keeping up with things. He'd stopped being a general naturalist and become a Fuzzyologist. Well, the Company's Science Center tried to keep up with everything. After lunch—well, say just before cocktail time, which would be just after lunch in Mallorysport—he'd screen Juan Jimenez and find out if anything unusual was happening.

The Fuzzy named Kraft—he was the male of the pair —wriggled in the little chair. The globe above and behind him glowed clear blue. Leslie Coombes sympathized with Kraft; he'd seen enough witnesses wriggling like that in the same kind of chair.

"You want to help Unka Ernst, Unka Less'ee," Ernst Mallin was pleading. "Maybe this is not so, but you say. You not, Unka Ernst, Unka Less'ee have bad trouble. Other Big Ones be angry with them."

"But, Unka Ernst," Kraft insisted. "I not break asht'ay, Unka Less'ee break."

The woman in the white smock said, "You tell Auntie Anne you break ashtray. Auntie Anne not be angry at you."

"Go ahead, Kraft. Tell Miss Nelson you broke ashtray," he urged.

"Come on, Kraft," Mallin's assistant said. "Who broke ashtray?"

The steady blue glow darkened and swirled, as though a bottle of ink had been emptied into it. There were brief glints of violet. Kraft gulped once or twice.

"Unka Less'ee broke asht'ay," he said.

The globe turned bright red.

Somebody said, "Oh, *no!*" and he realized that it was himself. Mallin closed his eyes and shuddered. Miss Nelson said something, and he hoped it wasn't what he thought it was.

"Oh, God; if anything like that happens in court . . ." he began. The red flush was fading from the veridicator globe. "You'd better send that veridicator to the shop. Or psychoanalyze it; it's gone bughouse."

"Unka Ernst," the Fuzzy was pleading. "Plis, not make do anymore. Kraft not know what to say."

"No, I won't Kraft. Poor little fellow." Mallin re-

leased the Fuzzy from the veridicator, hugging him with
a tenderness Coombes had never thought him capable
of. "And Auntie Anne not angry with Unka Less'ee.
Everybody friends." He handed Kraft to the girl.
"Take him out, Miss Nelson. Give him something nice,
and talk to him for a while."

He waited till she carried the Fuzzy from the room.

"Well, do you know what happened?" he asked.

"I'm not sure. We'll test the veridicator with a nor-
mally mendacious human, but I doubt if there's anything wrong with it. You know, a veridicator does not
actually detect falsification. A veridicator is a machine,
and knows nothing about truth or falsehood. You've
heard, I suppose, of the experiment with the paranoid
under veridication?"

"Got that in law-school psychology. Paranoid
claimed he was God, and the veridicator confirmed his
claim. But why did this veridicator red-light when Kraft
was telling the truth?"

"The veridicator only detects the suppression of a
statement and the substitution of another. The veridicator here had a subject with two conflicting statements, both of which he had to regard as true. We were
insisting that he confess to breaking that ashtray, so,
since we said so, it must be true. But he'd seen you
break it, so he knew that was also true. He had to suppress one of these true-relative-to-him statements."

"Well, maybe if he tries it again . . ."

"No, Mr. Coombes." Even Frederic Pendarvis ruling
on a point of law could not have been more inflexible.
"I will not subject this Fuzzy to any more of this. Nor
Ebbing. They are both beginning to develop psychoneu-
rotic symptoms, the first I have ever seen in any Fuzzy.
We'll have to get different subjects. How about your
defendants, Mr. Coombes?"

"Well, the test-witness isn't supposed to be a person
giving actual testimony. Besides, I don't want them
taught to lie and then have them do it on the stand. How

about some of the Fuzzies at Holloway's?"

"I talked to Mr. Holloway. While he's aware of the gravity of the situation, he was most hostile to using any of his own family, or Major Lunt's, or Gerd and Ruth van Riebeek's. He uses those Fuzzies as teachers, and lying isn't something he wants on the curriculum at Fuzzy school."

"No. I can see that." Jack wasn't the type to win battles by losing the war. "Have you no other Fuzzies?"

"Well, certainly Mrs. Hawkwood wouldn't want the ones I've loaned her for the schools trained in prevarication. And the ones I have helping with mental patients at the hospital have been successful mainly because of their complete agreement with reality. I don't know, Mr. Coombes."

"Well, we only have three weeks till the trial opens, you know."

xi.

Wise One was not happy. They had been in this place for four day-times and four dark-times, and none of the others wanted to leave. It was a good place, and he himself would have wanted to stay if it were not that he wanted more to go on to the Big One Place.

They had found it almost toward sundown-time on the day it had rained by following a little moving-water up the side of the mountain the way from which it came into a little valley that had been wide when they had first entered it and had become narrower as the mountain had grown steeper on either side. They had found a good sleeping-place where a tree had fallen in a small hollow beside a rock-ledge. Back under the ledge and the fallen tree the ground had been dry, although it had rained hard until sun-highest-time. They had gathered many ferns and had made a bed big enough for all of them together, and had made a place to put the bright-things so that they would not have to carry them when they hunted. After the first night, with the sleeping-place made, they played on the bank of the little moving-water until it became dark. There were good-to-eat growing-things nearby, and hatta-zosa among the trees below and on either side; and best of all, there were many zatku, more than anybody could remember. Last day-time they had found and eaten a whole hand and one finger of them, almost a whole zatku for each of them.

They had seen flying-things several times after they had crossed the moving-water to the sun's right hand. Always they had been far away, to sun-upward. They seemed to be going along over the great-great moving-water that went from the sun's left hand toward the sun's right hand. Big She and some of the others had been afraid and had hidden, but that had been foolish, for the flying-things were too far away for the Big Ones in them to see. Big She said they were hunting, and would eat them all if they found them. That was more of Big She's foolishness. The Big Ones were People, and People did not eat People. That was a foolish thing even to think about. Only gotza ate their own kind. And the Big Ones must hate gotza, for they killed them whenever they found them. But Big She and Stonebreaker and Fruitfinder, who listened to her, were afraid, and their foolish talk made the others afraid too.

Stabber was not afraid of the Big Ones, though. He had talked about how good it would be to find them and make friends with them, but the others had all cried out about that, and there had been the beginning of a quarrel. After that Stabber had kept quiet, except when the two of them were alone together.

They were together now along the moving-water below the open end of the little valley, looking for zatku and staying away from the places where the hatta-zosa fed, so as not to frighten them away. The others were all at the sleeping-place, resting and playing; they had hunted all morning and made a big hatta-zosa killing, and nobody was hungry. Stonebreaker was making another knife, better than the other one, and the rest were making telling-things with little stones on the ground about how many hatta-zosa they had killed and how many zatku. They would do that until near sundown-time, and then they would go out and hunt again. That was what they did each day.

It was nice to have a place like this, where they could rest and play all they wanted and not have to move all the time. Stabber was saying so now.

"Find place like this at Big One Place," Wise One told Stabber. "Maybe Big Ones have places like this. Go away far in flying-things to hunt, always come back to same place."

"You think Big Ones live across mountain?"

He nodded. "Maybe across other mountains, across many mountains. But Big Ones live to sun's left hand."

He was sure of that. He tried to think how he knew it, but that was harder. He pointed to the sun's right hand, to the line of mountains across the moving-water they had crossed a hand of days ago. Then he sat on the ground and picked up a stick and scratched a line with it.

"Moving-water we crossed at stony place; you remember?" Stabber, squatting beside him, did. "Goes that way, to great-great moving-water nobody can cross. Great-great moving-water goes to sun's right hand. Some place, far-far to sun's left hand, great-great moving-water little, like this, comes out of ground."

Stabber agreed. All moving-waters came out of the ground somewhere, that was an everybody-knows thing. Moving-waters became big because other moving-waters flowed into them. He scratched another line to show the great-great moving-water.

"Must be far-far, for great-great moving-water to get so big. Many little moving-waters come into it," Stabber considered.

"Yes. This place a nobody-know place. Nobody ever tell about it. Big Ones come from some place nobody ever tell about before. Far-far place. And flying-things come from sun's left hand. We know; we see."

"Big Ones must be very wise," Stabber said. "Go in flying-things, make thunder-death. I think flying-things made-things. Big Ones make like we make clubs, cutting-stones. I think Big Ones make bright things too."

He nodded. That was what he thought, too.

"Among Big Ones, we be like little baby ones," he said. "Not wise at all. People help little baby ones, teach them. Big Ones help us, teach us. Big Ones not let gotza, hesh-nazza catch us, eat us. Make gotza, hesh-nazza dead with thunder-death."

He looked out across the valley; he could see, far away, the ravine in the other mountain from which they had fled the hesh-nazza. Big Ones would not have fled; they would have made the hesh-nazza dead, and then cut it up and eaten it.

"But others, Big She, Other She, Stonebreaker, Fruit-finder, all afraid of Big Ones," Stabber said. "And not want to leave this place."

Then, he and Stabber would go alone. But he didn't want to leave the others; he wanted them to go along too. He looked at the mountains to the sun's right hand again.

"Maybe," he said hopefully, "Hesh-nazza come across moving-water. "Then all afraid to stay; want to go away."

"But hesh-nazza not cross. Water too deep, too fast. And hesh-nazza not able to go around, way we did," Stabber objected.

That was so. But he wished the hesh-nazza would come over to this side. They would all want to leave, especially Big She. If he could see it first and be able to warn them . . . Then a thought occurred to him.

"We go back to sleeping-place, now," he said. "We tell the others hesh-nazza come. We tell them we see hesh-nazza. Then they all want to go."

"But . . ." Stabber looked at him in bewilderment. "But hesh-nazza not here." He couldn't understand. "How we say we see hesh-nazza?"

It would be like the way he had told them about the long-ago People stories about the wonderful country to the sun's left hand. It would be a not-so thing, but he would speak as though it were so.

"You want to go to Big One Place?" he asked. "You want some go one place, some go other place, never see again? Then, we make others afraid to stay here. They not know we not see hesh-nazza. You think Big She go to look? You not make foolish-one talk!"

"Hesh-nazza not here, we tell others hesh-nazza here?" Stabber thought about it, realizing that it would be possible to do it. Then he nodded. "They not know. We tell them, they think hesh-nazza here. Come."

"Make run fast," he said. "Hesh-nazza chase us; we afraid."

They dashed among the others, shouting, "Hesh-nazza! Hesh-nazza come!" All the others, who were between the sleeping-place and the small moving-water, sprang to their feet. They all believed the hesh-nazza was upon them. Carries-Bright-Things ran and got the three sticks with the shining things on them; Stone-breaker caught up the chopper and the knife he had made and the knife on which he was working. Nobody wasted time on argument. They all scampered up the side of the little ravine away from the sleeping-place and the little moving-water. When they were out of the ravine, they all ran very fast, up the side of the mountain.

"Make hurry, make hurry!" he urged. "Not stop now. Maybe hesh-nazza come up here."

Hesh-nazza did that. Anything they could not catch by lying still and waiting they would try to catch by circling around. That was an everybody-knows thing. The ones who had begun to slow made haste again.

They all slowed down, however, as the trees ahead of them became thinner. Finally, near the top, they stopped, and kept still to listen. They could hear birds and small animals in the brush. Everybody relaxed; the hesh-nazza was not close now. Wise One was relieved too, until he remembered that there was no hesh-nazza. He had only said there was.

They came to the edge of the mountain. It fell away in

front of them, steeper and higher than the one they had
come down on the other side of the river. Below and beyond were no more big mountains, only small hills and
ridges, and there would be many moving-waters and
woods in which to hunt. Far away, so far as to be almost
as blue as the sky and hard to see against it, a high
mountain stretched away on both hands until it was beyond seeing. It was from this mountain, he was sure,
that the great-great river that flowed to the sun's right
hand came.

The others, even Big She, who had been complaining
because they had had to leave the nice place behind,
were crying out at the wonder of everything in front of
them. Then he saw a tiny brightness in the sky, so small
that he lost it when he looked away and had trouble
finding it again. Then, directly in front, he saw another.
At first he thought it was the first one, and wondered
at how fast it had moved, even for a Big Ones' flying
thing. But then he saw that it was another, and he could
see both of them. *Two* flying-things! He had never seen
more than one at a time.

Now he knew that he had been right all along. The
Big One Place *was* to the sun's left hand, perhaps just
over those high mountains in the distance.

xii.

Three days after the election, Gus Brannhard landed his aircar at Hoksu-Mitto at mid-afternoon. It had been a long time—since before the Pendarvis Decisions—since Jack had seen him in anything but city clothes. Now he was the old Gus Brannhard, in floppy felt hat, stained and faded bush jacket with cartridge-loops on the breast, hunting knife, shorts and knee-hose, and ankle boots. He got out of the car, shook hands, and looked around. Then, after dragging out a canvas kit bag and two rifle-cases, he looked around again.

"God, Jack, you have this place built up," he said. "It looks worse on the ground even than it did from the air. I hope you don't have all the game scared out of the country."

"For about ten, fifteen miles is all. George Lunt sends a couple of men out each day to shoot for the pot." He picked up the kit bag Gus had set down. "Let's get you settled and then have a look around."

"Any damnthings?"

"A few. The Fuzzies who come in at the posts to the south mention seeing hesh-nazza. We're not shooting any back of the house, the way I did in June. And we're not seeing any harpies anywhere, lately."

"Well, that's a good job!" Gus didn't like harpies either. Come to think of it, nobody did. "I'm going to

103

stay a couple of days, Jack. Maybe go out and pot a
zebralope, or a river-pig, tomorrow. Just take it easy.
Next day I'll go looking for damnthings."

Back in the living room, Jack got out a bottle. "It's
an hour till cocktail time," he apologized, "but let's
have a primer. On the election." He poured for both of
them, raised his glass, and said, "Cheers."

"I hope we have something to cheer about." Gus
lowered his drink by about a third. "We elected a hundred and twenty-eight out of a hundred and fifty delegates. That looks wonderful—on paper." He halved
what was left of his drink. "About forty of them we can
rely on. Company men and independent businessmen
who know where their business comes from. Another
thirty or so are honest politicians; once they're bought,
they stay bought. It's amazing," he parenthesized,
"how fast we grew a crop of politicians once we got
politics on this planet. As for the rest, at least they
aren't socialists or labor-radicals or Company-haters.
They're the best we could do, and I'm hoping, though
not betting, that they'll be good enough. At least there's
nobody against us with money enough to buy them
away from us."

"When'll the Convention be?"

"Two weeks from Monday. It'll be at the Hotel Mal-
lory; the Company's picking up the tab for the whole
thing. Starts with a banquet on Sunday evening. I know
what it'll be like. In the mornings they'll all be nursing
hangovers." Gus was contemptuous; he'd probably
never had a hangover in his life. "And in the evenings
they'll be throwing parties all over the hotel. We'll get a
couple of hours work out of them in the afternoons.
That may be all to the good." He looked at his empty
glass, then at the bottle. Jack pushed it across the table
to him. "You take any hundred and fifty men like this
Horace Stannery here, or Abe Lowther at Chesterville,
or Bart Hogan in the Big Bend district—I got him acquitted of a cattle-rustling charge a year and a half

ago—and every one of them'll try to show their constituents what statesmen they are by sponsoring some lamebrained amendment nobody else is witless enough to think of. That was a good constitution Leslie Coombes and I wrote. I hate to think of what it'll be like when it's adopted."

He finished his second drink. Before he could start on another, Jack suggested, "Let's go out and look around till the gang starts collecting."

They started down the walk toward the run. There were quite a few Fuzzies playing among the buildings, since it was late enough for them to have lost interest in lessons and drifted out of the school-hut. More had crossed the bridge to watch the fascinating things the Big Ones were doing around the vehicle park.

Two, both males, approached. One said, "Heyo, Pappy Jack," and the other asked, "Pappy Jack, who is Big One with face-fur?"

Gus laughed and squatted down to their level.

"Heyo, Fuzzies. What names you?"

They gave him blank stares. He examined the silver ID-disks at their throats. They were blank except for registration numbers. "What's the matter, Jack? Don't they have names?"

"Except the ones who want to stay here, we don't name them; we let the people who adopt them do that."

"Well, don't they have names of their own? Fuzzy names?"

"Not very good ones. Big One and Little One and Other One and like that. In the woods, mostly they call each other You."

Gus was scratching one on the back of the neck, which all Fuzzies appreciated. The other was trying to get his knife out of the sheath.

"Hey, quit that. Not touch; sharp. You savvy sharp?"

"Sure. Knife for me sharp, too." He drew it from the sheath on his shoulder bag and showed it: three-inch blade, which would be equivalent to nine-inch for a human. The edge was razor-keen; he'd been around here long enough to learn how to keep a knife honed. The other Fuzzy showed his too, and Gus let them look at his. It had a zarabuck-horn grip; they recognized that at once.

"Takku," one said. "You kill with noise-thing?"

"Big Ones," the other said reprovingly, "call takku zarabuck. Big Ones call noise-thing gun."

They tagged along, talking about everything they saw. Gus lifted them, one to each shoulder, and carried them. Taking rides on Big Ones was something all Fuzzies loved. They were still riding on Uncle Gus when they returned to the camp-house, where George Lunt and Pancho Ybarra were mixing cocktails and Ruth van Riebeek and Lynne Andrews were assembling snacks. Usually Fuzzies didn't hang around at cocktail time; this was when Big Ones wanted to make Big One talk. These two, however, refused to leave Gus, and sat with him on the grass, sipping hokfusinated fruit juice through straws.

"You're hooked, Gus," George Lunt told him cheerfully. "You're Pappy Gus from now on."

"You mean they want to stay with me?" Gus seemed slightly alarmed. He liked Fuzzies, the way some bachelors like children, as long as they're somebody else's. "You mean, all the time?"

"Sure," he said. "Little Fuzzy's been spreading the word; all the Fuzzies will have Big Ones of their own. They've picked you for their Big One."

"You be Big One for us?" one of the Fuzzies asked. They both lost interest in their fruit juice and tried to climb onto his back. "We like you."

"Well, mightn't be such a bad idea, at that," Gus considered. "I'm going to get a place of my own, out of town, say ten or fifteen minutes flying-time." With the kind of aircar he flew, and the way he flew it, that would be four or five hundred miles. "I like it where it gets dark at night, and if you want noise, you have to make it yourself.''

''I know.'' He looked around Hoksu-Mitto and thought of what Holloway's Camp had been like. ''It used to be that way here.''

The next morning, Gus was still in bed when Holloway went across the run to his office. He got through his paperwork in a couple of hours and then looked in at the school and at Lynne Andrews's clinic, dispensary, and hospital. Lynne had another viable Fuzzy birth to report, and was as proud as though she had accomplished it herself. That would be one of the first wave to get down into the Piedmont and cash in on the landprawn boom. The Fuzzy gestation period was a little over six months. It would be March or April at the earliest before the hokfusine-babies started coming in. Maybe, in time, they'd have a population explosion to worry about. Give that the Scarlett O'Hara treatment; enough other things to think about today.

He found Gus Brannhard on what passed for the lawn of the camp-house, playing with the two Fuzzies.

''I thought you were going hunting this morning.''

Gus looked up, grinning as sheepishly as his leonine features permitted.

''I thought I was, too. Then I got to playing with the kids here. Maybe I will this afternoon, but I just feel lazy.''

He just felt tired, was what. He'd been pushing himself hard; probably hadn't had two good nights sleep in a row since *People* versus *Kellogg and Holloway* had been scheduled for trial.

''Why don't you take the kids hunting? I think they'd like it.''

That hadn't occurred to Gus. ''Well, but they might get hurt. Or lost; mind, I'm going five, six hundred miles to hunt.''

''They won't get lost. When you set your car down, leave the generator on, on neutral. They can hear the vibrations for five or six miles; if you get lost, they'll lead you back. George Lunt's boys always do that when they go out with Fuzzies."

"Suppose I shoot something; won't that scare them?"

"Nah, they like shooting. They're always underfoot at the Protection Force target range. And I think you'll all three have fun."

"Hear that, kids? You want to go with Unka Gus, hunt takku, hunt . . . what the hell's the Fuzzy for zebralope?"

"Kigga-hikso."

"Zeb'alope? You shoot zeb'alope too?" the Fuzzies both asked.

Gus wasn't back till after the crowd began assembling for cocktails at the camp-house that afternoon; when he came in he set the car down in back of the cookhouse first, then brought it across the run and grounded beside the house. The Fuzzies jumped out at once, shouting, "Kill zeb'alope! Kill zarabuck! Unka Gus kill zeb'- alope, two zarabuck!"

Gus came over more slowly, unslinging his rifle, dropping out the magazine and clearing the chamber, picking up the ejected round. He was laughing as he leaned the rifle beside the bench at the kitchen door.

"Give me a drink, somebody. No, not that stuff; isn't there any unadulterated whiskey around? Thank you, George." He poured from the bottle Lunt gave him, took a big drink, and refilled his glass. "My God, you should have seen those kids! We set down beside a little creek a couple of miles above where it empties into Snake River. First of all, that one over there yelled, 'Zatku! Zatku!' and took off with his chopper-digger. The other one started circling around, and in a minute or so he had one. So we hunted zatku—land-prawn; goddamnit, as soon as you learn the native names for things, the natives start talking Lingua Terra. Then, after they killed a couple of them, they were after me,

'Pappy Gus, now we hunt zeb'alope.' So we hunted zebralope.

"They don't hunt by scent, like dogs, but they're the smartest trackers I ever saw. Look, you've hunted on Loki; so have I. You know how good the Bush Dwanga there are. Well, these Fuzzies could make the best Dwanga tracker I ever hunted with look like a blind imbecile. As soon as they find a fresh track, they split. One went one way, and the other another. In a minute, there was a big zebralope, damn near the size of a horse, running right at me. I gave him one in the shoulder and one in the neck; that finished him. So I gutted it. I knew they like raw liver, so I sliced the liver up for them. They wanted me to eat some. I told them Big Ones didn't like raw liver. Now they think Big Ones are all nuts. They ate the kidneys too. So then we hunted zarabuck. We got two. Your namesakes, Gerd; van Riebeek's zarabuck— the little gray ones."

"Did they eat the livers and kidneys from them too?" Lynne Andrews demanded. "You bring them around to the dispensary tomorrow."

"Well, there is one thing for damn-good-an'-sure: I'm adopting two Fuzzies. They're the best hunting companions I ever had. Beat a dog every way from middle; better hunters, and better company. You can talk to a dog, but a dog can't talk back to you, and Fuzzies can. Unka Gus and his Fuzzies are going to have a lot of fun. *Pappy* Gus," he corrected himself. "Pappy is the title of a Big One who stands *in loco parentis* to a Fuzzy; Unka just means *amicus Fuzziae* in general."

"What are you going to call them?"

"I don't know." Brannhard thought for a moment. "George named his crowd after criminals. Fitz Mortlake named his for detectives and spies. I'll have to name mine for hunters. Fiction-names: Allan Quartermain and Natty Bumppo. You hear that, kids? You have names now. Allan Quartermain name for you;

Natty Bumppo name for you. Now, I hope I don't forget which is which.''

The next day, he teleprinted the Fuzzies' registration numbers, fingerprints, and new names to Mrs. Pendarvis at the Adoption Bureau, so Gus Brannhard was now officially Pappy Gus. With some misgivings, Pappy Gus took Allan Quartermain and Natty Bumppo damnthing hunting. He carried his big double express, and took one of George Lunt's men, similarly armed, along. Damnthings were nothing for one man, or one man and two Fuzzies, to go after alone. The Fuzzies had excellent suggestions about how to find one, but they thought Pappy Gus and the other Big One were taking foolish chances to get out of the car and shoot it on foot.

"Thought I'd have some difficulty explaining that," Gus said when he returned. "Sportsmanship is not usually an aboriginal virtue. Put in the form of 'more fun,' though, they got it. I taught them how to shoot, too. They thought that was fun."

"Not with a 12.7 express, I hope."

"No, with my pistol." Gus's pistol was an 8.5-mm Mars-Consolidated, a hunting weapon with an eight-inch barrel and a detachable shoulder-stock. "It was too clumsy for them, but the recoil didn't bother them at all. I was surprised. I thought it'd kick hell out of them, but it didn't. They liked it."

Holloway was surprised too. He'd thought that even a .22 would be too much for a Fuzzy.

"I'm going to have Mart Burgess make up a couple of little rifles for them," Gus was saying. "Eight-point-five pistol, say about four pounds. Single-shot, at least for their first ones. Too many complications about an auto-loader for a Fuzzy to remember."

If anybody could make a Fuzzy-size rifle, Mart Burgess could. He was the same sort of gunsmith as Henry Stenson was an instrument-maker. You only found that sort of craftsmanship on low-population planets where there was no mass market to encourage mass production. Holloway didn't quite like the idea, though.

"All the other Fuzzies'll hear about it, and they'll want rifles too. You give rifles to primitive peoples, you know what happens? Teach these Fuzzies about bows, and they can make their own, the way the Fuzzies are doing here. Give a Stone Age people steel spears and knives and hatchets, and one will last years. As soon as they learn blacksmithing they can make their own out of any scrap they pick up. But give them firearms, and they have to have ammunition. They can't make that themselves; they're past the point of no return. The next thing, they forget how to use their own weapons, and then they really are hooked."

Gus said the same thing Pancho Ybarra had said a couple of weeks ago.

"They're hooked now, on hokfusine, even if they don't know it. They can't get enough from land-prawns.

"And talk about being hooked, how about yourself? You don't make your own ammunition; you even stopped reloading because it was too much bother. What *do* you use that you make yourself?"

"That's different. I trade for what I use. It used to be sunstones; now it's the work of running this madhouse. With you, it used to be defending criminals, and now it's prosecuting them. But we both trade, and the Fuzzies haven't anything to trade. What they get from us is free handouts."

"Like Nifflheim they haven't anything to trade. You mean to sit there and tell me you don't get anything from Little Fuzzy and Mamma Fuzzy and Baby and the rest of your family? If you don't, why don't you get rid of them? You think Victor Grego doesn't get something from that Fuzzy of his? Why, he'd kill anybody who tried to take Diamond away from him. Or my Allan and Natty, that I've only had since yesterday?

"You talk about anybody being hooked; *we're* hooked. Hooked on Fuzzies. And they earn everything they get from us just by being around. You just let them keep on being Fuzzies, and don't worry about anything else. They'll be all right as long as we're all right to them."

xiii.

Two days later Gus Brannhard went back to Mallory-sport, taking Allan Quartermain and Natty Bumppo along, all three happy. The other Fuzzies were all happy too; envy, like lying, was a vice Fuzzies didn't have. There was a big crowd of them to see their friends off, and Jack watched them break into little groups to return to play or lessons, all talking about how nice it was for Natty and Allan, and how soon they'd all have Big Ones of their own, too. He went back across the run to his office.

There was more topographic data and detail-maps of the country north of the Divide sent down from Yellow-sand Canyon. Everybody had known, in general, what the country was like up there, mostly from telescopic observations made on Xerxes Naval Base. What they were getting now was low-level air-survey stuff, mostly of the Yellowsand River and the Lake-Chain River which joined it from the west. This, of course, didn't show how many Fuzzies there were up there, or where. Not many, he supposed, and it'd be a Nifflheim of a job contacting them.

He got his hat and went out, crossing the run again. The schoolhouse was relatively quiet. There was a small class in progress, run by Syndrome and Calamity Jane and a couple of the new teaching Fuzzies, on how to

make talk in back of mouth like Big Ones. Ruth van
Riebeek and Mamma Fuzzy and Ko-Ko and Cinderella
were running a class in Lingua Terra—"Big Ones not
say zatku, say lan'-p'awn." Fuzzies, he noticed, had
trouble with r-sounds, and consonant-sounds following
other consonants. Three more were doing blacksmith
work. They had some photocopied pictures from some
book on ancient pregunpowder weapons, of Old Terran
English bills and Swiss halberds. They were making a
halberd now with a steel staff. Wooden staves were too
flimsy for their strength, or else too awkwardly thick.
Outside, there was shouting mixed with yeeks.

He went out the other end of the hut, trailing pipe-
smoke, and found fifty or sixty of them at archery prac-
tice, waiting their turns to shoot at a life-size and not
implausible-looking padded and burlap-covered figure
of a zarabuck. Gerd van Riebeek was acting as range officer, with Dillinger and Ned Kelly and Little Fuzzy and
Id coaching. One Fuzzy, his feet apart, drew his arrow
to his ear and loosed it, plunking it into where the zarabuck's ribs would have been. Before it landed, he had
another arrow out of his quiver and was nocking it.

"Anybody seen the High Sheriff of Nottingham
around anywhere?" Gerd asked. "He better get on the
job, or the king'll be fresh out of deer."

The second arrow went into the burlap zarabuck at
the base of the neck. More names for Fuzzies—Robin
Hood, Friar Tuck, Little John, Will Scarlet. . . .

A zarabuck would feed the average Fuzzy band for
two days, or a double band for a day, and the woods
were lousy with zarabuck. More meat to a kill would
mean that Fuzzies could operate in larger bands. And a
zarabuck-hide would make three or four shoulder bags,
not as good as the waterproof, zipper-closed, issue-type,
but good enough to carry things; and Fuzzies needed
some way to carry things. He remembered the pitifully
few possessions Little Fuzzy's band had brought in with
them; and by Fuzzy standards they'd been rich. Usually,

a band would have only their clubs, and maybe a flake knife or a *coup-de-poing* axe. At bottom, any culture was a matter of possessions—things to do things with. Everything else—law, social organizations, philosophy —came later.

Robin Hood, or Samkin Aylward, or whoever he was, had shot his third arrow; he and all the others bolted down the hundred yards to the target. It was a miracle, the way those kids had picked archery up; less than a month, and it would take a couple of years to make that kind of archers out of humans. A Fuzzy in the woods, with a bow, could eat mighty well. Fifteen or twenty Fuzzies with bows wouldn't have any trouble at all keeping everybody well-fed, all the time. They could make permanent homes, and wouldn't have to be on the move all the time. That might be the way to handle it: a string of Fuzzy villages all through the Piedmont, with patrol cars dropping in every couple of days to keep them supplied with hokfusine. Maybe big villages, with a ZNPF trooper as permanent resident.

And, what the hell, give them rifles and ammunition. An 8.5-mm high-speed pistol cartridge would kill a zara-buck; Gus Brannhard had potted quite a few with his Mars-Consolidated. Even kill a harpy; and a couple of 8.5's in the right places would make a damnthing lose interest in Fuzzy for dinner. So, they'd need ammunition. Well, they needed hokfusine anyhow, and a case of cartridges now and then wouldn't make much difference. One thing, needing cartridges they'd stay around where they'd get hokfusine too.

The next day, Victor Grego dropped in en route to Yellowsand, accompanied by Diamond. After saying hello to all his human friends in sight and asking Pappy Vic's permission, Diamond went off with Little Fuzzy to see the sights.

"How many Fuzzies do you have now?" Grego asked, as he and Jack strolled toward the schoolhouse.

Jack told him, around five hundred. Like everybody else, Grego thought that was a hell of a lot of Fuzzies in one place. Well, damn it, it was, and there didn't seem to be much that could be done about it.

"Coming in, I saw a couple of hundred of them along Cold Creek, below where the run comes in," he added. "Had some fires going, and there were a couple of lorries grounded with them. More of your gang?"

"Oh, yes. That's the shipyard and naval academy. We're teaching them how to build rafts and paddle and steer them. Rivers give Fuzzies a lot of trouble; a river like the main Snake or the Blackwater's bigger to a Fuzzy than the Amazon on Terra or the Fa'ansare on Loki is to us. That's why we get so many of them here; the river systems to the north funnel a lot of them down Cold Creek."

"This crowd doesn't need to build rafts anymore. They've made it on their own. They've joined the Human-People now."

And he couldn't take them back and dump them in the woods; he realized that now. The vilest cruelty anybody can commit is to give somebody something wonderful and then snatch it away again.

"I don't know what the Nifflheim I'm going to do with them," he admitted. "It'll depend on how this minor-child status holds up, for one thing."

"We can get that written into the Constitution," Grego said. "That's if we can get it adopted after we write it in."

They had almost reached the schoolhouse. He stopped short.

"You think there's any doubt?" he asked.

"Well, you know what kind of a goddamn rabble of delegates we have; fifty or sixty we can depend on, and it takes a two-thirds vote to adopt a constitution. The rest of that gang would sell us out for a candy-bar."

"Well, give them a candy-bar. Give them two candy-bars, and a gold-plated eight-bladed Boy Scout knife."

He repeated what Gus Brannhard had said about no opposition with money enough to buy them away from the
Company and the Government.

"That's what I'm worried about. Hugo Ingermann,"
Grego said. "I know what he wants to do in the long
run. He wants to wreck the Company and Ben Rainsford's Government, both, and build himself up on the
ruins. That People's Prosperity Party looks dead now,
but those things are as hard to kill as a Nidhog swamp-
crawler, and just as poisonous. What he wants is to get
an anti-Company Constitution adopted, and then get an
anti-Rainsford Legislature elected."

"How much money has he?" Jack started Grego
away from the schoolhouse and in the direction of his
office across the run. Whatever this was, he wanted to
talk it over privately. "And is he spending any?"

"He's not spending any we know of, but he's borrowing all over the place. You know that North Mallorysport section?"

That had been one of Grego's few mistakes. About
ten years ago there had been a brief flurry in private in-
dustry, and the Company had sold land north of the
city. Now it was a ghost town, abandoned factories and
warehouses, and a ruinous airport. Hugo Ingermann
had managed to acquire title to most of it.

"He's borrowing on that, every centisol he can. Need-
less to say, we're buying the mortgages from the bank.
In non-Company hands, that place could be made into
a planetside spaceport to compete with Terra-Baldur-
Marduk on Darius, and we don't want that. He's been
getting the money in cash or negotiable Banking Cartel
certificates; none of it's deposited. The people at the
bank say he's all but cleaned out his accounts there. I
don't know what he wants with all that loose cash, and
not knowing bothers me. He hasn't been spending any
of it we can find out about."

That meant not spending any, period; the Company's
investigators found things out quickly. They went over

to the office and kicked it around from every angle they could think of, and neither of them kicked any enlightenment out of it. Hugo Ingermann was up to something, and they didn't know what, and neither of them liked not knowing. They didn't talk about it with the others at cocktail-time; they talked about the Fuzzies and what they could do with any more of them.

"Why don't you plant Fuzzy colonies on the other continents?" Grego asked. "We have a lot of good Fuzzy country we'll lease back to the Government at one sol for value received, or something like that. If this hokfusine program works the way everybody expects it to, we'll have Fuzzies all over everything."

That was a good idea. Something else to think about tomorrow and do something about after the Fuzzies' legal status was determined.

In the evening, just before Fuzzy bedtime, Little Fuzzy and Diamond approached him and Grego.

"Pappy Jack," Little Fuzzy began, "Diamond want me to go visit with him, at Pappy Vic place, where Big Ones dig. Say much fun there."

"You want, Pappy Vic?" Diamond asked. "Little Fuzzy come with us, make visit. Then, we go home, bring Little Fuzzy back here."

"What do you think, Jack?" Grego asked. "I'll bring him back in a couple of days, and it'll be a lot of fun for both of them. Diamond's never had a friend with him at Yellowsand. I know, there's a lot of blasting and digging and so on, but he won't get hurt. I'll look after him, and so'll Diamond. Diamond knows what's dangerous and what isn't."

Diamond must have been telling him all about Yellowsand, and he wanted to go see and come back and tell about; sure. And Grego was always back and forth between Mallorysport and Yellowsand, and he always took Diamond with him; he wouldn't do that if there were any real danger. Besides, there'd been enough digging and bulldozing and construction-work around here for Little Fuzzy to know what to watch out for.

"Yes; you go with Diamond; see Pappy Vic place; have plenty fun," he said. "But you be good Fuzzy; do what Pappy Vic, Diamond say; not do anything they say not do. You listen to Diamond; he know about digging-place."

"Nobody get hurt if watch out," Diamond said. "Pappy Vic tell me all about things that hurt; I tell Little Fuzzy. We have much fun."

xiv.

Little Fuzzy was excited and happy. He always liked to go for trips, and this was a trip to a new place he had never seen before, a place called Yellowsand. That meant *Rohi-Nasig*; it would be a sandy place, like beside a river. At this place, Pappy Vic and other Big Ones were digging the top off a mountain and throwing it down in a deep-place, to get bright-stones out of black hard-rock. All Big Ones wanted bright-stones because they were pretty, and Pappy Vic traded them with other Big Ones, and part of what he traded for was nice things to give to the Fuzzies. Pappy Jack and Pappy Gerd had found this place, and now it belonged to Gov'men'; that was why all the Big Ones made their name-marks on the papers that time at Pappy Ben Place.

Pappy Vic sat in front, making the aircar fly; Little Fuzzy and Diamond were on the back seat, looking out the windows. They were high up; they could see everything spread out below, just like the make-like-country things Pappy Jack had, the *maps*. He could see where he and the others of his band had come down from the sun's right hand, the *north*, hunting land-prawns, for many-many days, between new-leaf time and ground-berry-time, before he found Wonderful Place and got into it and made friends with Pappy Jack. He saw the river that had been too big to cross, and remembered

how they had gone to sun-downward, *west*, along it for
many days before it was small enough to go over.

If only they had known how to build the rafts the way
Pappy Jack and Pappy Gerd and Unka Pancho showed
them! But now they didn't need rafts. The Big Ones
would take them in aircars, high over all the rivers and
mountains; why, it had taken more days than he could
count to come south to Wonderful Place, and now they
were flying over it before one could make talk about it.

"Look far-far ahead," Diamond told him. "See
mountains go from west to east?" Diamond knew the
Big One words; Pappy Vic had taught him. "Yellowsand there. Soon see everything, then go down, go on
ground."

There was an aircar ahead, a green one; it was one
that Pappy George's blue-clothes police went about in.
Maybe they were hunting harpies; they killed many harpies with big shoot-fast guns. Pappy Vic made talk with
whoever was in it, with the talk-far things, the *radio*.
They passed over a mountain; it was not steep as they
approached, but it dropped sharply on the other side.
Then he knew they were far-far to the north. He remembered this kind of mountain. There was a river on the
other side, and another mountain, rising gradually and
dropping sharply on the other side, and another mountain beyond that. Beyond the far mountain was a yellow
haze. Diamond saw it and pointed excitedly.

"Is Yellowsand, Pappy Vic digging-place!" he said.
"Is dust. Much dust where Big Ones dig."

"You kids, look out right window," Pappy Vic said.
"I go around, so you see from high-up. Then go out
over mountain, come up deep-down place."

Pappy Vic made the aircar come down a little and go
slowly. They passed over the mountain, with Diamond
beside him pointing. There were two rivers back of this
mountain; they ran together, and where they made one
was a split place in the mountain beyond, and they ran
into it. And there was Yellowsand, Pappy Vic's place; it

was much bigger than Wonderful Place. There were at least a hand of hands of houses . . . what was the Big One word for that many? *Twenty-five.* The Big Ones had names for how many anything was, even the leaves on a big tree. And he could see the deep place where the two rivers made one and ran out through the mountain, and beside this the Big Ones were working, many-many of them, with many-many machines; digging machines and picking-up machines and ground-pushing machines and big carry-things aircars.

Pappy Vic must have many-many friends, to come and help him dig like this, and more were coming, because they were building more houses. Everybody must like Pappy Vic.

Pappy Vic took the car out over the top of the mountain, and Little Fuzzy was surprised. He had thought that there would be a valley and another mountain sloping up beyond, but there was not. The mountain went almost straight down, very-very far, and beyond it was flat country, with little hills, and then bigger hills until he could see no farther. Pappy Vic made the car go down beside the face of the mountain till they were almost at the bottom, and then turned and went to where the mountain was split and the river came out of it. He looked up through the hard see-through stuff on the top of the car, amazed at how far it was up to the top. If he saw nothing else, this alone was worth coming to see.

The river came out so fast that it was foaming white; on either side were beaches of sand, and he could see why the Big Ones called this place Yellowsand; beyond the beaches trees grew back to where the mountain started to go up. Nobody could cross this river, not even Big Ones, not even with rafts.

"Bad place," Diamond told him. "Not go near. Get in river, make dead right away."

"That's right, Little Fuzzy. Don't go near that river at all," Pappy Vic said. "And look ahead, there."

There was a falling-water. He had seen falling-waters before, but never one so high as this. Even inside the car he could hear it; it was loud like thunder all the time. And far above, big carry-things aircars were coming out over the deep place and dumping loads of rock and ground and even whole trees that had been dug up by the roots. Pappy Vic made the aircar go straight up so that they could watch the falling-water until they were up above the top.

Then they went over the place where all Pappy Vic's friends were digging for him, and he looked down, watching all the work that was going on, until the car came down among the bright metal houses, in front of one big one, and there was a hand or so of Big Ones waiting for them. They all wore clothes like Pappy Jack wore when he was at home at Wonderful Place, except two, whose names were Chief and Captain, who wore blue police clothes, and all carried one-hand guns, like the Big Ones at Wonderful Place. They were all nice.

Pappy Vic showed him where he and Diamond would sleep, and he left his chopper-digger there, though he kept his shoulder bag. Then Pappy Vic took him and Diamond out to look at the digging-place. Diamond had seen it many times before; he explained all about it, how they had to take the soft yellow rock off the top of the black hard-rock, and then crack up the hard-rock to find the shining stones inside. It was interesting to watch how they did it, and he saw a wonderful thing, a wide moving-strip, like the moving-strips and the moving-steps inside buildings in Big House Place, only much bigger, which carried the black hard-rock into a place with strong wire fence all around.

Pappy Vic took him and Diamond into this place. Here the hard-rock was cracked, and the shining stones gotten out. There were many-many Big Ones working at this. Also, there were many police-clothes Big Ones, with one-hand guns on their belts, and little two-hand shoot-fast guns, all standing around watching. They must be afraid that bad Big Ones would come and try to take the shining stones. And he saw the place where the shining stones were sorted out. They were very pretty, all bright like fire. No wonder they had to be careful nobody would take pretty-things like that.

Then they went back to the big metal house, and it was lunchtime. They gave him and Diamond estee-fee to eat. For a long time after lunch Pappy Vic and the others made talk. It was Big One talk, and Little Fuzzy understood very little of it, but it seemed to be about the work that was being done here. He and Diamond played on the floor, and he smoked his pipe. Diamond didn't smoke; he didn't like it.

In the afternoon, Pappy Vic took them up in an aircar to watch his friends making blast. He knew all about that. The Big Ones put something in the ground and got far away from it, and it went off like a gun only much-much louder, and there was smoke and dust and big rocks flew high up. It made digging easier, but it was dangerous to be close to it; and, while Big Ones didn't mind it, it made bumps in the ground that hurt Fuzzies' feet. That was why Pappy Vic took him and Diamond up in the aircar while it was happening. As soon as the blasts were done, the Big Ones all moved in again with their machines and started digging.

Pappy Vic took him and Diamond back to the big metal house, and they ate more estee-fee, and played with Diamond's things. And then it was Diamond's nap-time, and he lay down on his blankets and went to sleep.

Little Fuzzy lay down beside Diamond and tried to sleep too, but he couldn't. He was too excited about all the things he had seen. He thought about all Pappy Vic's friends helping him dig, and all the machines they had to work with, and then he thought about all the pretty shining-stones he had seen, all the colors there were, and bright like hot coals in a fire. He wanted a shining-stone himself, to take back to Wonderful Place and show to the others there.

He knew that Pappy Vic would give him one if he asked for it, but Pappy Jack had told him that he must never ask people for things when he was away from home. Well, maybe he could find one for himself. Of course, all the shining-stones here belonged to Pappy Vic, but if he found one himself and asked if he could keep it, that would be different from asking for one Pappy Vic had found. He thought of asking Diamond about this, but Diamond was asleep, and it was never right to bother people who were sleeping unless something was wrong or there was danger.

So he decided to go out by himself and look for one. He put on his shoulder bag and picked up his chopper-digger, because he might find a land-prawn, and went out, going in the direction of the edge of the deep-place, away from where the Big Ones were working. He found much black-rock in a place where they had been digging a little once and had stopped, and looked all around, but he found no shining-stones. Maybe they had found all the shining-stones that were here. He went to the edge of the deep place and looked down, and away down at the bottom he saw more black-rock.

He knew that Pappy Vic and Diamond had both said that he was to stay out of the deep-place, but this was far away from where the Big Ones were throwing the top of the mountain down into it; it would not be dangerous here. He started to climb down.

It was hard climbing, and much farther down than he had thought, and several times he was tempted to turn back, but he could see black-rock at the bottom and kept on. He wanted to find a shining-stone for himself. There was much loose rock, and he had to be careful where he put his feet. He had to use his chopper-digger to help him and cling to small bushes that grew on the steep side of the deep-place, and there were bushes and even trees that had been dug up and thrown over when the Big Ones had been digging above. He had to be very careful among them.

Finally, he was down to the very edge of the river; it was fast and foamed among rocks, and he began to wish he had not come down here. The black hard-rock he found was all broken into little pieces, none bigger than his body, and he knew now that there would be no shining-stones. He knew what the Big Ones did; they broke the black-rock small and put a thing Pappy Vic called a scanner on the pieces, and it told if there were shining stones inside.

For a moment he looked at the broken black-rock, and then he said, "Sunnabish-go-hell-goddamn!" He didn't know what these words meant, but Big Ones always said them when things went wrong. Then he started along the edge of the river, looking for a less steep place to go up again, farther away from where Pappy Vic's friends were throwing rock down. Looking around, he saw a nice flat rock, and another rock just above it, and a bush he could hold to above that.

He jumped down from the uprooted tree onto which he had climbed, onto the flat rock. As soon as his feet touched it, the other rocks around him were sliding, too. He struggled to regain his balance, and the chopper-digger flew out of his hand; he heard it fall with a clink among the rocks above him. Then he was sliding toward the river, and he was more frightened than he had ever been, even when a bush-goblin had almost caught him long ago—and then he was in the water.

Something heavy hit him from behind. He clutched at it. . . .

xv.

Jack Holloway leaned forward for his tobacco pouch, his eyes still on the microbook-screen. The Fuzzies on the floor in front of him were also looking at the screen, yeeking softly to one another; they had long ago learned not to make talk with Big One voices around Pappy Jack when he was reading. They were reading, or trying to, too; at least, they were identifying the letters and spelling out the words aloud, and arguing about what they meant. They probably missed Little Fuzzy; whenever they were stumped on anything, they always asked him. Jack blew through his pipe stem, and began refilling the pipe from the pouch.

The communication-screen buzzed. He finished refilling the pipe and zipped the pouch shut. The Fuzzies were saying, "Pappy Jack; screeno." He said, "Quiet, kids," and snapped it on. As soon as they saw Victor Grego's face in it, they began yelling, "Heyo, Pappy Vic!"

"Hello, Victor." Then he saw Grego's face, and stopped, apprehension stabbing him. "What is it, Victor?" he asked.

"Little Fuzzy," Grego began. His face twitched. "Jack, if you want a shot at me, you're entitled to it."

"Don't talk like a fool; what's wrong?" By now, he was frightened.

Grego said, "We think he's gone into the river," as though every word were being pulled out of him with red-hot pincers.

Jack's mind's eye saw the Yellowsand River rushing down through the canyon. He felt a chill numbness spread through him.

"You 'think.' Aren't you sure? What happened?"

"He's been missing since between 1530 and 1700," Grego said. "He and Diamond lay down for a nap in the afternoon. When Diamond woke, he was gone; he'd taken his shoulder bag and his chopper-digger with him. Diamond went out to look for him, and couldn't find him. He came back while some of us were having cocktails and told me. I supposed he'd just gone out to look for a land-prawn, but I didn't want him running around the diggings alone. Harry Steefer called the captain on duty at the police hut and had a general alert put out—just everybody keep an eye open for him.

"He didn't show up by dinner-time, and I began to get worried. I ordered a search and took Diamond up in a supervisory-jeep, with a loudspeaker to call him, and we hunted all over the area. Diamond assured me that he'd warned him against going down in the canyon, but we began looking there. After it got dark, we put up lorries with floodlights in the canyon. Maybe I should have called you then, but we were expecting to find him every minute."

"Wouldn't have done any good. I couldn't have done anything but worry, and you were doing that already."

"Well, about half an hour ago, a couple of cops in a jeep were going along the edge of the river, and one of them saw a glint of metal among the rocks. He looked at it with binoculars, and it was Little Fuzzy's chopper-digger. He called in right away. I went down; I've just come back from there. That's all there was, just the chopper-digger. The place is all loose rock that's been thrown down from above; it's right under where we made one of the prospect digs. We think the loose rock started to slide and he threw the chopper-digger out of his hand, trying to catch himself, and the slide took him down . . . Jack, the whole damn thing's my fault. . . ."

"Oh, hell; you couldn't keep him on a leash all the time. You thought he'd be all right with Diamond, and Diamond thought he was going to take a nap too, and . . ." He paused briefly. "I'm coming up right away; I'll bring some people along. That river's a hell of a thing for anybody to get into, but he might have gotten out again." He looked at the clock. "Be seeing you in about an hour."

Then he screened Gerd van Riebeek, who was getting ready for bed, and told him. Gerd cursed, then repeated what he had been told over his shoulder to Ruth, who was somewhere out of screen-range.

"Okay, I'll be along. I'll call Protection Force and have Bjornsen and the rest of the gang who were up there with me called out; they know the place. Be seeing you."

Then Gerd blanked out. Jack kicked his feet out of his moccasins and pulled on his boots, buckled on his pistol and got his hat and a jacket. There was a kitbag ready, packed for emergencies. Weather forecast hadn't been good; southwest winds, with a warm front running into a cold front at sea to the west. He got a raincape too. He only had to wait a few minutes before Gerd was at the door. Ruth was with him.

"I'll Fuzzy-sit, and put them to bed," she said. "Or maybe they'd like to come down to our place for tonight." He nodded absently, and she continued: "Jack, maybe he's all right. Fuzzies can swim when they have to, you know."

Not in anything like Yellowsand Canyon. He wouldn't bet on a human Interstellar Olympic swimming champion in a place like that. He said something, he didn't know what, and he and Gerd hurried to the hangar and got his car out.

After they were airborne, he wished he hadn't let

Gerd take the controls; flying the car would have given him something to concentrate on. As it was, all he could do was sit while the car tore north through the night.

In about ten minutes they began running into cloud—that rain the forecast had warned of. They got below the clouds. Maybe they were flying through rain now; an aircar at Mach 3 could go through an equatorial cloudburst on Mimir without noticing it. He could see lightning to the northwest, and then to the west. Then there was a blaze of electric light on the under side of the clouds ahead.

It was drizzling thinly when they set down at the mining camp at Yellowsand. Grego was waiting for him, so was Harry Steefer, the Company Police chief who had transferred his headquarters to Yellowsand when the mining had begun. They shook hands with him, Grego hesitantly.

"Nothing yet, Jack," he said. "We've been over that canyon inch by inch ever since I called you. Just nothing but that chopper-digger."

"Victor, you're not to blame for anything. If blaming anybody means anything. And Diamond's not to blame, and I don't even think Little Fuzzy's too much to blame. He wanted to see what it was like down there, and maybe he thought he'd find a zatku. Aren't many zatku around Hoksu-Mitto anymore." Hell, he wasn't talking to Grego, he was talking to himself. "Hirohito Bjornsen's on his way, with the gang he had here before you took over."

"He's not in the canyon at all; we're sure of that. We're looking along both banks below, but I don't think he got out of it. Not alive."

"I know what it's like. Hell, I discovered it. Now I wish I hadn't."

"Jack, I'd give every sunstone in this damned mountain if . . ." Grego began, then stopped, as though it were the most useless thing in the world to say, which it was.

Bjornsen arrived with a combat car and two patrol cars. George Lunt was along, and so was Pancho Ybarra. They spent the night searching, or drinking coffee in the headquarters hut, listening to reports and watching screen-views. The sky lightened to a solid dull gray; finally the floodlights went off. The rain continued, falling harder, a constant drumming on the arched roof of the hut.

"We've been halfway to the mouth of Lake-Chain River," Bjornsen reported. "We didn't see anything of him on either side of the river. If the visibility wasn't so bad . . ."

"Visibility, what visibility?" a Company cop wanted to know. "Anything down there I can see, I can hit with a pistol, the way the fog's closing in."

"Damn river's up about six inches since midnight," somebody else said. "It'll keep on rising, too." He invited them to listen to that obscenely pejorative rain.

Jack started to yawn and bit on his pipe stem. Grego, across the rough deal table, was half-asleep already, his head nodding slowly forward and then jerking up.

"Anybody fit to carry on for a while?" he asked. "I'm going to lie down; wake me up if anybody hears anything."

There were a couple of Army cots at the end of the hut. He rose and went toward them, unbuckling his belt as he went, sitting down on one to pull off his boots. He was about to stretch himself out when he remembered that he still had his hat on.

xvi.

At first, Little Fuzzy was only aware of utter misery. He was cold and wet and hungry, and he hurt all over, not in any one place but with a great ache that was all of him. It was dark, and rain was falling, and all around him he could hear the gurgling rush of water moving, and, finding that he was clinging tightly to something, he clung tighter, and felt the roughness of bark under his hands. His knees were locked around something that must be a tree branch, and he wondered how he had come here.

Then he remembered—hunting for shining-stones where the Big Ones had been digging, going down into the deep-place beside the river; he wished he had listened to Pappy Vic and Diamond and stayed out of there. Falling into the water. He remembered clutching something that had hit him in the water, and he remembered the small tree that the Big Ones had uprooted and thrown down over the edge. It must have gone into the water when he did.

Then everything had gone black, and he had known nothing more, except once, for just a little, he had seen the sky, with black clouds angry-red at the edges, and once again it had been dark and he had seen lightning. It had been raining then.

But the tree was not moving now. He thought he knew

what had happened; the river had carried it against the bank and it had stopped. That meant that he could get onto ground again. He clutched tighter with his hands and loosened his knee-grip, putting one foot down and touching soft ground with it. He decided to remain where he was until it became light enough to see before he tried to do anything. Then, gripping tightly with his knees and one hand, he felt to see if he still had his shoulder bag. Yes, it was there. He wanted to open it to see if water had gotten into it, but decided not to until it was light again. He wriggled to make himself more comfortable, and went back to sleep.

It was daylight when he woke. Not whole daylight, and it was still raining and there was a fog, but he could see. The river, yellow and rapid, rushed past on both sides. The tree was caught on a small sandbar, and there was water on both sides of it. A little grass grew on the sandbar, and there were bits of wood that the river had left there at other times, and a whole big tree, old and dead. Climbing off the little tree, he walked about until some of the stiffness left his muscles.

He would have to get off this sandbar soon. The rain was still falling, and when it rained rivers became more, and this river might come up over the sandbar before long.

On one side, the river was wider than he could see in the fog; on the other, the left side as it flowed, it was not much more than a stone-throw to the bank, and the bank looked low enough for him to climb up out of the river. He picked up some bits of wood and threw them in the water to test the current. It was faster than he liked, but he noticed that the wood was carried toward the bank. He threw in many sticks, watching how each one was carried. Then, making sure that the snaps that held his knife and trowel in their sheaths were closed, he waded into the water. As soon as he was carried off his feet, he began swimming against the current.

He was carried downstream a little, but always in the

direction of the bank, and soon his feet touched bottom. He struggled out of the water and up onto the bank, and then looked back at the sandbar he had left. "Sunnabish river," he said.

It was still raining, but he was so wet that he did not notice it. He was tired, too; it had been a hard swim, even that little distance. The river was very strong; it made him happy that he had fought it and won. Then he walked to a big tree and sat down on an exposed root, opening his shoulder bag. Everything in it was dry; not a drop of water had gotten in. He had a cake of estee-fee; he broke it in half, put one half back in, and then ate half of the other. Maybe he would not be able to find anything to eat before he would be hungry again. It made him feel good. Then he put away what was left and got out his pipe and tobacco and lit it. Then he took out the flat round thing that had the blue pointer-north in it, the compass, and looked at that. The river flowed almost straight north; that was what he had expected. Then he looked at the other things he had.

Beside his pipe and tobacco and the lighter and the compass, there was a whistle. He blew that several times. That was a good thing to have. Maybe he could use it to call attention to himself if he saw a Big One far away. He put it away, too. And he had his knife and his trowel, and he had the little many-tool thing which the nice Big One with the white hair had given him in Big House Place. It had a knife in it too, a small one, very sharp, and a pointed thing to punch, and a bore-holes thing, and a file, and a saw, and a screwdriver, and even a little thing in two parts that would pinch like the jaw of a land-prawn and cut wire. And he had wire, very fine but strong—one had to be careful, or it would cut— and a ball of strong string, *fishline* the Big Ones called it, and short pieces of string that he had saved. He always carried plenty of string; it had many uses.

He finished his pipe, and wondered if he should smoke another, then decided not to. He had plenty of tobacco, but he must not waste it. He didn't know how long it would take to get back to Yellowsand. If he followed this river, he would get there sooner or later, but it might be a long way. The river had been very fast, and he had been in it on the tree a long time. And when he got to where it came out of the mountain, he would have the mountain to climb. He wasn't going into the deep-place again, he was sure of that.

He wished he had his chopper-digger; he would have to kill animals for food on the way. At first, he thought of making himself a wooden prawn-killer, but decided not to, at least now. So he found three large stones, smooth and rounded, each bigger than his fist. One he carried in his hand, and the other two he carried in the crook of his other elbow. He started north along the bank of the river.

Once, he saw a big bird in a tree, its head under its wing. It was too far to throw; he wished he had one of the bows Pappy Jack and Pappy Gerd had taught how to make, and some arrows. That bird would have been good to eat. He wished he were back at Hoksu-Mitto, with Pappy Jack and Mamma and Baby and Mike and Mitzi and Ko-Ko and Cinderella . . . and Unka Pancho, and Auntie Lynne, and Pappy Gerd and Mummy Woof, and Id and Superego and Complex and Syndrome, and . . . as he walked, he said all the names of all his friends at Hoksu-Mitto, wishing that he was with them again.

Sometime, he thought, after sun-highest time—*noon, lunchtime*—he saw a zarabunny sitting hunched into a ball of fur. It didn't like the rain any more than he did. He hurled a stone and hit it, and then ran to it before it could get up, and stabbed it in back of the ear with his knife. Then he squatted and skinned it. At first, he thought of making a fire and cooking it on a stick, but it would take too long to find dry wood and make the fire and cook it, and he was hungry again. He ate it raw. After all, it had only been very short time that he had eaten anything at all that had been cooked.

One thing, he would have to make himself better weapons than stones to throw.

The third time he came to a stream and crossed over it, he found hard-rock, not black like the shining-stone-rock of Yellowsand, but good and hard. He hunted until he found two pieces the right size and shape, and put them in his shoulder bag. By this time, the rain had stopped and it was getting foggier and darker, and he thought that dark-time was near.

He made a sleeping-place in the next hollow, beside a stream and against the side of a low cliff. First he found a standing dead tree and cut at it with his knife until he had cut off all the wet wood and made fine shavings of the dry wood. These he lit, and put sticks on the fire; as they dried, they caught, until he had a good fire, warm and bright. By this time it was growing dark, and the fire made light on the rocks behind him. He gathered more wood, some pieces so big that he could hardly drag them, and stacked it where the fire would dry it. He did this till it was too dark to see, and then he sat down with his back to the rocks and took the two pieces of flint out of his shoulder bag.

One, he decided, would be an axe: he could chop wood with it for other fires and kill land-prawns with it. The other would be the head of a spear, which he could throw or stab with. For a long time he looked at the stone, making think-pictures of what the axehead and the spearhead would be like when he had finished them. Then he took out his trowel, which had a handle of made-stuff, *plastic,* and began pressing with it on the edge of the stone. The stone gouged and scarred the plastic, but the rock chipped away in little flakes. Now and then he would lay it aside and go to put more wood on the fire. Once, he heard a bush-goblin screaming, far away, but he was not afraid; the fire would scare it away.

The spearhead was harder to do. He made it tapering

to a point, sharp on both edges, with a notch on either side at the back; he knew just how he was going to fasten it to the shaft. It took a long time, and he was tired and sleepy when he had finished it. Laying it and the axehead aside, he put more wood on the fire and made sure there was nothing between it and him, so that it would not spread and burn him, and curled up with his back to the rock and went to sleep.

The fire had burned out when he woke, and at first he was frightened; a bush-goblin might have come after it had gone out. But the whole hollow smelled of smoke, and bush-goblins could smell much better than people. The smoke would be frightening in itself.

He dug his hole with the trowel and filled it in; he drank from the little stream, and then ate what was left of the half cake of estee-fee he had eaten the day before. Then he found a young tree, about the height of a Big One, and dug it up with his trowel and trimmed the roots to make a knob. The other end he cut off an arm's length from the knob and split with his knife and fitted the axehead into it and made a hole in it below the axehead with his bore-holes thing. He passed wire through that and around on either side of the stone, many times, until it was firm and tight. Pappy Jack and Pappy Gerd and the others said this should be done with fine roots of trees, or gut of animals, but he had no time to bother with that, and wire was much better.

Then, with the axe, he cut another young tree, slender and straight. The axe cut well; he was proud and happy about it. He fitted the shaft to the spearhead, using more wire, and when that was done he poked through the ashes of the fire, found a few red coals, and covered them with his trowel. Pappy Jack and Pappy George and Pappy Gerd and everybody always said that it was a bad never-do-thing to go away and leave a fire with any life in it. Then, making sure that he had not forgotten any of his things, he picked up his axe and spear and started off through the woods toward the big river.

A little before noon he found another zarabunny, and threw the spear, hitting it squarely. Then he finished it with a chop on the neck. That made him happy; he had used both his new weapons, and they were good. He made a small fire here, and after it had burned down to red coals he put the back-meat of the zarabunny on sticks and cooked it, as he had learned at Hoksu-Mitto.

Pappy Jack was wise, he thought, as he squatted beside his little fire and ate the sweet hot meat. He had wondered why Pappy Jack had insisted that all Fuzzies learn these things about living in the woods, when they would have Big Ones to take care of them. *This* was why. There would be times like this, when Fuzzies would lose their Big Ones, or become lost from them, just as he had. Then they could do things like this for themselves.

He decided not to eat all the zarabunny. He had taken the skin off carefully; now he wrapped what was left of the back-meat and the legs in it, and tied it to his shoulder bag. He would cook and eat that when he made camp for the night.

The fog was still heavy, with thin rain sometimes. He made camp this time by finding two big bushes with forks about the same height and cutting a pole to go between them. Then he cut other bushes to lean against that, and branches to pack between. There were ferns here, and he gathered many of them, drying them at the fire and making a bed of them. He was not so tired today, and all the soreness of his muscles had gone. After he had cooked and eaten part of the zarabunny, he smoked his pipe and played with some pebbles, making little patterns of what he had done that day, and then went to sleep.

It was still foggy and rainy the next morning. He cooked one of the hind legs of the zarabunny that he had saved, and then killed the red coals left of his fire

and went on. Toward the middle of the morning,
he found a land-prawn and chopped off its head and
cracked the shell. He did not make a fire for this; land-
prawns were best raw; cooking spoiled the taste. Big
Ones ate many things without cooking them, too.

About the middle of the afternoon, he found a goofer
chewing the bark off a tree. This was wonderful luck—
meat for two whole days. He threw the spear and caught
the goofer behind the shoulder with it, and then used the
axe to finish it. This time he did build a fire, and after
he had gutted the goofer, he began to think about how
he would carry it; it weighed almost as much as he did.
He decided not to skin it here. Instead, he spitted the
liver and the kidneys and the heart, all of which were
good, and roasted them over the fire. After he had eaten
them, he cut off the head, which was useless weight, and
propped the carcass up so that the blood would drain
out. When this was done, he tied each front and hind leg
together with string, squatted, and got the whole thing
on his back, the big muscles of the hind legs over his
shoulders. It was heavy, but, after he got used to it, it
was not uncomfortable.

Some time after this, when he was close to the river,
he saw through the fog where another river came into it
from the east; it was a big river too. After that, the river
he was following was less because it had not yet been
joined by the other one. This was good, he thought. It
looked not much bigger than it had when it had come
out of the deep place in the mountain. He must be getting close to Yellowsand. He was sure that if it had not
been for the fog he could have seen the big mountains
ahead.

He made camp that night in a hollow tree which was
big enough to sleep in, after cooking much of the
goofer. He ate a lot of it; he was happy. Soon he would
be back at Yellowsand and everybody would be happy
to see him again. He smoked a second pipe before he
went to sleep that night.

The next day was good. The rain had stopped and the fog was blowing away, and there was a glow in the sky to the east. Best of all, he could hear the sound of air-cars very far away. That was good; Pappy Vic and his friends had missed him and were out hunting for him. The sound was from away down the river, though, and that wasn't right. He knew what he would do; he would stay as close to the river as he could. If they saw him, they would come and pick him up; then he wouldn't have to climb the high-steep mountain. Maybe, if he found a good no-woods place, he would build a big fire beside the river. They would be sure to see the smoke.

The sounds of the aircars grew fainter, and finally he couldn't hear them at all. He found another land-prawn and ate it. This was the fourth day since he had been in this place, and he had only found two of them. He knew that land-prawns were more to the south, but he was surprised at how few there were here.

The wind blew, and then it began to rain some more. It often did this before the clouds all went away. But the rain came from in front of him and to the left, and before it had come from the right. The wind could have changed, but this troubled him. Finally, he looked at his compass, and saw that he was not going north at all, but west.

That wasn't right. He got out his pipe; Pappy Jack always smoked his pipe when he wanted to think about something. At length, he walked over to the river and looked at it.

With all the sand from Yellowsand, it should be yellow, but it wasn't; it was a dirty brown-gray. He looked at it for a while, and then he remembered the other river he had seen coming in from the east. That was the river that came out of the mountain at Yellowsand, not this one.

"Sunnabish!" he almost yelled. "Jeeze-krise go-hell goddamn sunnabish!" That made him feel a little better, just as it did the Big Ones. "Now, must go back." He thought for a moment. No, it was no use going back; he could not cross this river where it met the other one. He would have to go all the way up this go-hell river till he could find a place to cross, and then all the way down again. "Sunnabish!"

xvii.

None of them said anything much. Grego and Harry Steefer and the rest were the kind of people who always got sort of tongue-tied when it came to verbal sympathy. Come right down to it, there wasn't a Nifflheim of a lot anybody could say. Jack shook Grego's hand with especial warmth. "Thanks for everything, Victor. You all did everything you could." He and Gerd van Riebeek turned away and went to the aircar.

"You want to fly her, Jack?" Gerd asked.

He nodded. "Might as well." Gerd stood aside, and he got in at the controls. Gerd climbed in after him, slamming the door and dogging it shut, then said, "Secure." He put the car on contragravity and fiddled with the radio compass; when he looked out, Yellowsand was far below and he could see out into the country beyond the Divide. The scarps of the smaller ranges to the south rose, one behind the other, on the other side.

"Maybe we ought to have stayed a little longer," he said. "It's starting to clear now; all blue sky to the south. Be clear up here by noon."

"What could we do, Jack? The Company cops and survey-crews are ready to throw it in now. So's George and Hirohito. If there'd been anything to find, they'd have found it."

"You don't think we'll ever find him?"

"Do you, Jack?"

"Oh, Gerd, he might have gotten out again. The current could have carried him to the side. . . ." He used an obscenity like an eraser on his previous words. "Who the hell do I think I'm kidding beside myself? If he isn't in the North Marsh by now, it's because his body's caught on a snag and being sanded over." He was silent again. "Just no more Little Fuzzy." He repeated it again, after a moment: "No more Little Fuzzy."

They were all angry with him, Stonebreaker and Lame One and Fruitfinder and Other She and Big She—especially Big She. Even Stabber and Carries-Bright-Things were not speaking for him.

"Look at place Wise One bring us!" Big She was railing. "Wise One tell us, to sun's left hand is good place, always warm, always good-to-eat things. This is what Wise One say; Wise One not know. Wise One bring us to this place. Big moving-water, not cross. Rain make down, rain make down, make wet, all time cold. Not find good-to-eat things, everybody hungry. And look at moving-water; how we cross that?"

"Then we go up moving-water, find place to cross. And rain stop some time; rain always stop some time," he said. "Is everybody-know thing."

"You not know," Lame One said. "This is different place. Maybe all time rain here."

"You make fool-talk. Rain all time, water everywhere."

"Much water here," Other She said. "Big wide water-places. Maybe much rain here."

"Sky look brighter," Stabber remarked. "Wind blow, too. Maybe rain stop make down soon."

And the gray not-see was gone, too; soon the rain would stop and the sun would come out again. But how to get across this big water? The moving-water was wide and deep, there were no stony places; it was a bad not-cross moving-water, and there were all the big widewaters, and it would be far-far to where they would be able to cross over.

"Hungry, too," Fruitfinder complained. "Not eat since long time before last dark-time."

He was hungry himself. If he had been alone, he would have gone on, hoping to find something, until he was able to cross the moving-water. None of the others, not even Stabber, would do that, however. They wanted to eat now.

"Animals stay under things, stay out of rain, not move about," he said. "Be where brush is thick. We go hunt different places. Anybody kill anything, bring back here, all eat."

They nodded agreement. That was the way they did it when it was best not to hunt all together. He thought for a moment. He didn't want Big She and Fruitfinder and Stonebreaker hunting together. They would all the time make talk against him, and when they came back they would make bad talk to the others.

"Stabber, you, Big She, go that way." He pointed down the river. "Take care, not get in bad not-go-through place. Lame One, you, Other She, Stone-breaker, go up moving-water. Carries-Bright-Things, Fruitfinder, come with me. We go back in woods. Maybe find hatta-zosa."

They were all angry with him because it had rained and because they had come to this big not-cross moving-water, and because they had found nothing to eat. They blamed him for all that. It was hard being Wise One and leading a band. They all praised Wise One when things went well, but when they didn't they all blamed him. But when he told them how to hunt, they all agreed. They had to have somebody to tell them what to do, and nobody else would.

. . . *beginning of a new era for our planet,* the smooth, ingratiating voice came out of thousands of telecast-speakers all over Zarathustra, in living rooms and cafés, in camp bunkhouses and cattle-town saloons. *Already, Mallorysport assumes a festive air in preparation to greet the Honorable Delegates to the Constitutional Convention which will begin its work a week from today.*

There is a note of sadness, however, to mar our happy enthusiasm. Word from the CZC camp at Yellowsand is that the search for Little Fuzzy, lost, presumably in the torrent of Yellowsand River, has been definitely called off; no hope remains of finding that lovable little person alive. A whole planet mourns for him, and joins with his human friend and guardian, Jack Holloway, in his grief.

Good-bye, Little Fuzzy. You were only with us a short while, but Zarathustra will never forget you.

xviii.

Little Fuzzy said, "Sunnabish!" again, in even deeper disgust. He relighted his pipe, but after two puffs it went out; there was nothing but ashes in it. He blew through the stem and put it away. There was no use making a big fire here; Pappy Vic and his friends were looking for him along the other river, the one that came out from Yellowsand. He couldn't even hear the aircar-sounds anymore. And all the way he would have to go, up this river and then down again . . .

"Jeeze-krise!"

Why hadn't he thought of that before? No, he wouldn't have to do all that! He would make a raft, the way he had been taught. Why, he had even helped teach others to do it. Then he would go down this river until he came in sight of the other river, and work over to the right bank. Then he would be close to Yellowsand and along the river where they were looking for him. As soon as he got on land again, he would make a big fire and right away somebody would see and come for him.

He couldn't do it here. The banks were too high, and if he made a raft he would never be able, alone, to get it down. So he would have to go up this river, but only till he found a good place, with the banks low, where there was wood to make the raft and the kind of trees that had fine, tough roots to twist into rope to tie the raft

together. And before he started to work on the raft he
would have to hunt for a while to get meat to eat while
he was working.

He scuffed dirt over the ashes he had knocked from
his pipe, picked up his axe and spear, and started off up
the river. After a while, the river turned south a little,
and then it became very wide. He stopped and looked: a
big lake. That was good. There would be low places
along it and the water would be still; he could build the
raft right in the water. The sun was beginning to come
out now, not brightly, but growing steadily brighter. He
was feeling very happy; building the raft was going to be
much fun.

Then he stopped short and said a number of the Big
Ones' angry-words, but even that didn't make him feel
better. In front of him the ground dropped off in a cliff,
as high as one of the big metal houses at Wonderful
Place. Beyond he could see flat ground full of trees and
bushes and tangled vines, with water everywhere. There
was a small stream at the foot of the cliff, and it spread
out all over everything. This was a bad sunnabish not-
go-through place; he would have to go up the little
stream to get around it. How far up the river it went he
had no idea. He looked at his compass again, saw that
the small stream went almost due north, and started up
along it.

The sun was out brightly now, and there were many
big blue places in the sky and the clouds were white
instead of gray. He walked steadily, looking about for
things to eat and looking at his compass. Finally he
came to where the stream ran over stones, and the
water-everywhere place had stopped.

He crossed over and went west, looking often at his
compass and remembering which way the big river was.
He heard noises ahead, and stopped to listen, then was
very happy because it was the noise of goofers chewing
at tree-bark. He went forward carefully and came upon
five of them, all chewing at trees. He picked out the

plumpest of them, drew back his arm, and threw his spear; it was not a very good throw because it caught the goofer through the belly, just back of the hips, from one side to the other. As he ran forward to finish it, another, frightened, ran straight at him. He hit it between the eyes with the axe; it died at once. He hadn't meant to kill two goofers, but a frightened goofer would attack a person. Then he finished the one he had wounded with his spear and pulled the spear out. The other goofers had all run away.

He gutted both of them, took out the livers and hearts and kidneys, and spitted them on sticks he cut with his knife. Then he built a fire. When he had a good bed of red coals he propped the sticks against stones and weighed them with other stones and sat down to watch that the meat didn't burn. It was very good.

He cut off the head of one goofer and made a pack of the carcass, as he had the one he had killed the day before. The other he skinned and cut up and wrapped the hind legs and the back-meat in the skin and tied that to the whole one. This was going to be a heavy load, but he thought he could manage it. He started off again. He didn't bother looking for good-to-eat things anymore; he had already eaten, and he had a whole goofer and the best meat of another. Even if he had seen a land-prawn, he wouldn't have bothered with it. He turned south; now he had the sun, and didn't need to bother getting out his compass.

Then, in front of him, he saw a splash of blood, and then places where the dead leaves were scuffed and more blood, and goofer-hairs with it. Somebody had been going in the direction of the river, dragging a dead goofer. That meant that there was a band of People about who had split up to hunt and would meet again somewhere. People hunting in a band would never drag a dead goofer; they would eat it where they had killed it. He went forward along the drag-trail, and then stopped.

"Heyo!" he shouted, as loudly as he could, then re-

membered that that was a Big One word, and these
People had never seen a Big One. He had also been putting his voice in the back of his mouth, to make talk like
a Big One. "Friend!" he shouted naturally, as he always
had before he had been taught. "You want make talk?"

There was no answer; they were too far ahead to hear.
He hurried forward, following the trail as fast as he
could. After a while, he shouted again; this time there
was an answering shout. He could see the big river
through the trees ahead, and then he saw three People
beside it. He hurried to them.

They were two males and a female. They all had
wooden weapons, not the paddle-shaped prawn-killers
the People in the south carried, but heavy clubs
knobbed on one end and pointed on the other. One of
the females also carried three small sticks in her hand.
On the ground was a dead goofer, the hair and skin
rubbed off the back where it had been dragged.

"Friend," he greeted them. "You make friends,
make talk?"

"Yes, make friends," one of the males said, and the
other asked, "Where from you come? Others with
you?"

He swung the load from his shoulders, the whole
goofer and the meat of the other, beside the goofer they
had, to show that he would share and eat with them,
and untied the strings and put them in his shoulder bag.
The others looked at these things and at his weapons in-
tently, but said nothing about them, waiting for him to
show and explain about them. The female said, "You
carry all that? You strong."

"Not strong; just know how," he replied. "Alone.
Come from far-far place, sun's left hand. Four dark-
times, fall in big river." Then he remembered that river
was not a Fuzzy word. "Big-big moving-water," he explained. "Catch hold of tree floating in moving-water,
hold onto. Moving-water take me far to sun's right
hand before I can get out. Walk back to place where can

cross. What place you come from?''

One of the males pointed northward. "Come many-many days," he said. "Band all come together." He held up a hand with five fingers spread, then lowered and raised it with three fingers extended. Eight of them. "Others hunt, some this way, some that way. Come back here, all eat together."

"We call him Wise One," the female said, pointing to the one who had spoken. "He called Fruitfinder," she introduced the other male. "Me Carries-Bright-Things." She held out the three sticks. "Look, bright-things. Pretty."

On the end of each stick was a thing he knew. They were the things that flew out when Big Ones shot with rifles. Empty cartridges. One was the kind for the rifles the blue-clothes police Big Ones had; Pappy Gerd had a rifle like that too. The other two cartridges were from a rifle like one of Pappy Jack's.

"Where you get?" he demanded, excited. "Are Big One things. Big Ones use in long thing, point with both hands. Pull little thing underneath, make noise like thunder. Throw little hard thing very fast; make dead hesh-nazza. You know where Big Ones are?"

"You know about Big Ones?" Wise One was asking just as excitedly. "You know where Big One Place is?"

"I come from Big One Place," he told them. "Hoksu-Mitto, Wonderful Place. I live with Big Ones, all Big Ones my friends." He began naming them over, starting with Pappy Jack. "Many Fuzzies live with Big Ones, can't say name for how many. Big Ones good to all Fuzzies, give nice things. Give shoddabag, like this." He displayed it. "Give knife, give trowel for dig hole bury bad smells. Teach things." He showed the axe and spear. "Big Ones teach how to make. I make, after get out of big moving-water. And Big Ones give Hoksu-Fusso, Wonderful Food."

There was shouting from up the river. The male Fuzzy who was called Fruitfinder, examining the axe, said, "Stabber, Big She come." Wise One began shouting, "Make hurry fast! Wonderful thing happen!"

Two more Fuzzies came out of the woods, dragging another dead goofer between them—a female with a club like the others' and a male with a sort of spear-stick. Carries-Bright-Things and Fruitfinder ran to help them, jabbering in excitement.

"Is somebody from Big One Place," Carries-Bright-Things was saying. "Is Big Ones' Friend. Knows what bright-things are."

The male with the spear-stick immediately began shouting at the female with him, "You see? Big Ones good, make friends. Here is one who knows. Wise One right all time."

"You show us way to Big One Place?" Wise One was asking. "Big Ones make friends with us?"

"Big Ones friends for all Fuzzies," he said, and then remembered that that was another Big One word. There were so many Big One words these Fuzzies did not know. "Fuzzy what Big Ones call all People like us. Means Fur-All-Over. Big Ones not have fur, only on head, sometimes on face." He decided not to try to explain about clothes; not enough words. "Big Ones very wise, have all kinds of made-things. Big Ones very good to all Fuzzies."

Three more came in. They had two zarabunnies and two land-prawns. Everybody was excited about that, and cried, "Look, two zatku!" Land-prawns must be very few in this place. It took a long time to tell these new ones, and the others, about the Big Ones and about Wonderful Place. He showed all the things he had in the shoulder bag, and the spear and axe he had made. Stabber seemed to think the spear was especially wonderful, and they all thought the shoulder bag itself was the most wonderful thing he had—"Carry many things; not have to hold in hand; not lose,"—but there were so many wonderful things to look at that none of them could think of any one thing long. He had been like that when he had first come to Wonderful Place, when Wonderful Place had been little and nobody but Pappy Jack had been there.

There was arguing among them, and he listened and thought he understood how things had been in this band. Wise One and Stabber had wanted to find the Big One Place and make friends with the Big Ones, and Big She and Fruitfinder and Stonebreaker had been afraid. Now everybody was siding with Wise One and mocking Big She, and even she was convinced that Wise One had been right, but didn't want to admit it. Finally, they all squatted in a ring, passing all his things around to look at, and he told them about the Big Ones and Wonderful Place.

What he wanted to know was how these people had found out about the Big Ones in the first place. It was hard to find this out. Everybody was trying to talk at once and not telling about things as they had happened. Finally Wise One told him, while the others kept quiet, at least most of the time, about the thunder-death that had killed the three gotza, and finding the tracks and where the aircar had been set down, and the empty cartridges. That had been Pappy Jack and Pappy Gerd; they had been to the north on a trip, and everybody at Wonderful Place had heard about the shooting of the three harpies. And they told about the flying thing, the aircar. That would have been Pappy Vic's friends or some of Pappy George's blue-clothes police people.

All the time, the sun was getting lower and lower toward its sleeping-place; soon it would be making colors. Finally, about Big Ones' koktel-drinko time, everybody realized that they were hungry. They began talking about eating, and there was argument about whether to eat the land-prawns first or save them for last.

"Eat zatku first," Stabber advised. "Hungry now, taste good. Save for last, not hungry, not taste so good."

Wise One approved that, and Big She agreed. Wise One cracked the shells and divided the meat among everybody. That showed how scarce land-prawns were here. In the south, nobody did that. Everybody killed and ate land-prawns for himself; there were enough for everybody. He told them so, and they were all amazed, and Stabber was shouting. "Now you see! Wise One right all the time. Good Country to sun's left hand, plenty everything!" Even Big She agreed; there was no more argument about anything now.

After they had eaten the zatku—he must remember to use only Fuzzy words, till he could teach the Big One words—they were ready to eat the hatta-zosa and the ho-todda. When they saw how he skinned and butchered with his knife, they wanted him to prepare all of them; all they had was one little stone knife.

"Not eat right away," he told them. "Cook first."

Then he had to explain about that, and everybody was frightened, even Wise One. They knew about fire; lightning sometimes made it, and it was a bad thing. He remembered how frightened he had been when he had first seen it in Pappy Jack's viewscreen. He decided, with all the meat they had, to make *barba-koo*. They watched him dig the trench with his trowel and helped him get sticks to put the hatta-zosa on and gather wood for the fire, but when he went to light it they all stood back, ready to run like Big Ones watching somebody making ready for blast.

But when the barba-koo was started, they came closer, all exclaiming at the good smells, and when the meat was done and cool enough to eat, everybody was crying out at how good it was. Little Fuzzy remembered the first cooked meat he had eaten.

By this time the sun was making colors in the west, and everybody said it was good that the rain was over. They all wanted to go find a sleeping-place, but he told them that this would be a good enough place to sleep,

since the rain was over and if they kept a fire burning all
the big animals would be afraid. They believed that;
they were still afraid themselves.

He got out his pipe and filled and lighted it, and after
a few puffs he passed it around. Some of them liked it,
and some refused to take a second puff. Wise One liked
it, and so did Lame One and Other She and Carries-
Bright-Things, but Stabber and Stonebreaker didn't.
They built the fire up and sat for a long time talking.

He needed this band. With eight beside himself, they
could build a big raft, and with eight and himself to
hunt they would not be hungry. He had to be careful,
though. He remembered how hard it had been to talk
the others into going to Wonderful Place after he had
found it and come back to get them to come with him.
They would make him leader instead of Wise One, but
he didn't want that. When a new one came into a band
and tried to lead it, there was always trouble. Finally he
decided what to do.

He took the whistle out of his bag and tied a string to
it long enough to go around the neck, and made sure
that it was tied so that it would not come loose. Then he
rose and went to Wise One.

"You lead this band?" he asked.

"Yes. But if you can take us to Big One Place, you
lead."

"No. Not want. You lead. I just show how to go.
Others know you, not know me." He took the whistle
—Wise One had learned how to blow it by now—and
hung it around his neck. "I give; you keep," he said.
"You leader; when band not together, want to call
others, you blow. When somebody lost, you blow."

Wise One blew piercingly on the whistle. A Big One
would have said, "Sank-oo," for a gift like this. Fuzzies
did not say such things; everybody was good to everybody.

"You hear?" he asked. "When I make noise like this,

you come. That way, nobody get lost.'' He thought for a moment. ''I lead band, but Big Ones' Friend know better than Wise One; he very wise Wise One. Wise One listen when he say something. All listen when Big Ones' Friend say anything, do as Big Ones' Friend say. That way, we all come to Big One Place, to Hoksu-Mitto.''

xix.

Gerd van Riebeek dropped his cigarette butt and heeled it out. A hundred yards in front of him a blue and white Extee Three carton stood pin-cushioned with arrows and leaking sand. There were almost as many arrows sticking in the turf around it, most of them very close. The hundred-odd Fuzzies were enthusiastic about it.

"Not good," he told them. "Half not hit at all."

"Come close," one of the Fuzzies protested.

"You hungry, come close not give meat. You not put come-close on stick, put over fire, cook."

The Fuzzies all laughed; this was a perfectly devastating sally of wit. A bird, about the size of a Terran pigeon, flew across the range halfway to the target. Two arrows hit it at once and it dropped.

"Now that," he said, "was good! Who did?"

Two of them spoke up; one was his and Ruth's Superego, and the other was an up-to-now nameless Fuzzy who had come in several weeks ago. Robin Hood would do for him. Then he looked again. No. Maid Marian.

That was with half his mind. The other half was worrying about Jack Holloway. Jack seemed to have stopped giving a damn after he came back from Yellowsand. If it only hadn't been Little Fuzzy. Any of the others, even one of his own family, he'd just have written off, felt badly about, and gotten over. But Little

Fuzzy was something special. He was the first one, and besides that, he had something none of the others had, the something that had brought him into Holloway's Camp alone to make friends with the strange Big One. Ruth and Pancho and Ernst Mallin hadn't gotten a dependable IQ-test for Fuzzies developed yet, but they all claimed that Little Fuzzy was a genius. And he was Pappy Jack's favorite.

And now Jack was drinking, too. Not just a couple before dinner and one or two in the evening. By God, he was drinking as much as Gus Brannhard, and nobody but Gus Brannhard could do that and get away with it. Gerd wished he'd gone along with Jack to Mallorysport, but George Lunt hadn't been away from here since right after the Fuzzy Trial, and he was entitled to a trip to town; and somebody had to stay and mind the store, so he'd stayed.

Oh, hell, if Jack needed looking after, George could look after him.

"Pappy Gerd! Pappy Gerd!" somebody was calling. He turned to see Jack's Ko-Ko coming on a run. "Is talk-screen! Mummy Woof say somebody in Big House Place want to make talk."

"Hokay, I come." He turned to the Protection Force trooper who was helping him. "Let them go get their arrows. If that carton doesn't fall apart when they pull them out, let them shoot another course." Then he started up the slope toward the lab-hut, ahead of Ko-Ko.

It was Juan Jimenez, at Company Science Center. He gave a breath of relief; Jack hadn't gotten potted and gotten into trouble.

"Hello, Gerd. Nothing more about Little Fuzzy?" he asked.

"No. I don't think there is anything more. Jack's in town; did you see him?"

"Yes, at the grand opening of the Fuzzy Club yesterday. Ben and Gus want him to stay over till the convention opens. Gerd, you were asking me about ecological side effects of harpy extermination and wanted me to let you know if anything turned up.''

"Yes. Has anything?''

"I think so. Forests & Waters has been after me lately. You know how all those people are; they get little, manageable problems, and never bother consulting anybody, and then when they get big and unmanageable they want me to work miracles. You know where the Squiggle is?''

He did. It was along the inside of the mountain range on the lower western coast. It wasn't really a badland, but it would do as a reasonable facsimile. Volcanic, geologically recent; a lot of weathered-down lavabeds covered with thin soil; about a thousand little streams twisting every which way and all flowing finally into the main Snake River from the west. Flooded bank-high in rainy season and almost dry in summer, doing little or nothing for the water situation on the cattle ranges at any season. For the last ten years, since the Company had been reforesting it, it had gotten a little better.

"Well, all those young featherleaf trees,'' Jimenez said, "they'd been doing fine up to a couple of years ago, holding moisture, stopping erosion, water table going up all over the western half of the cattle country. Then the damned goofers got in among them, and half the young trees are chewed to death now.''

That figured. They'd shot all the harpies out of the southern half of the continent long ago; first chased them out of the cattle country to protect the calves, and then followed them into the upland forests where they'd been feasting on goofers. Now the surplus goofers were being crowded out of the uplands and down into the Squiggle. Up in the north, Fuzzies killed a lot of goofers, but there were no Fuzzies that far south.

But why shouldn't there be?

"Juan, I have an idea. We have a lot of Fuzzies here who are real sharp with bows and arrows. I was out run-

ning an archery class when you called me; you should
see them. Say we airlift about fifty of them down to
where the goofers are worst, and see what they do.''

"Send them to Chesterville; the chief forester there'll
know where to spot them. How about arrows?''

"Well, how about arrows? How soon do you think
you can produce a lot, say a couple of thousand? I'll
send specs when I know where to send them. You can
make the shafts out of duralloy, the feathers out of
plastic, and the heads out of light steel. They won't have
to shoot through armor-plate, just through goofers.''

"Well, I wouldn't know about that; that's purely a
production problem. . . .''

"Then, talk to a production man about it. Is Grego in
town? Talk to him; he'll get your production problems
unproblemed.''

"Well, Gerd, thanks a million. That may just be the
answer. Airlift them around from place to place and
just let them hunt. I'll bet they'll get more goofers in a
day than five times as many men would get with rifles.''

"Oh, hell, don't thank me. The Company's done a
lot of things for us. Hokfusine, to put it in one word. Of
course, we'll expect the Company to issue the same
rations they're getting here. . . .''

"Oh, sure. Look, I'll call Victor. He'll probably call
you back. . . .''

xx.

Wise One was happy. For the first time since Old One had made dead, he did not have to think all the time of what to do next and what would happen to the others if anything happened to him. Big Ones' Friend would think about all that now; he was leading the band. Of course, he insisted that Wise One was the leader, but that was foolishness.

Or maybe it wasn't; maybe it was wisdom so wise that he thought it was foolishness because he was foolish himself. That was a thought he had never had before. Maybe he was getting wiser just by being with Big Ones' Friend. Big Ones' Friend didn't want to make trouble in the band; that was why he said Wise One should lead and had given the—the *w'eesle*—to show it. His fingers went to his throat to reassure himself that he really had it.

Then he squirmed comfortably among the dry soft grass and ferns under the brush shelter Big Ones' Friend had shown them how to make, with the warmth and glow of the fire on him, listening to the wind among the trees and the splashing of the little moving-water and the sound of the lake behind him. Fire was wonderful when one learned how to make it and how to keep it safe. He had been afraid of it; all the People, all the *Fuzzies*—he must remember that—were, but when one

knew about it, it was good. It frightened all the big
animals away. It made warmth when one was cold. It
made meat many-many times better.

But best of all, it made light in the dark. Look, here
were Other She and Carries-Bright-Things and Fruitfinder, beside the fire, twisting longleaf-tree roots to
make . . . to make *rope*—that was a Big One word. The
People, *Fuzzies,* had no word for it because they had
never known of it. It was long after dark. Without fire
they would all have been asleep long ago. And Stonebreaker was working too, making the chopping-stones
to put on sticks. It was strange that nobody had thought
of doing that before, or of putting pointed stones on
longer sticks to stab with. That made killing hatta-zosa
—*goofers*—much easier; Stabber and Lame One had
killed four today, after sun-highest time, *noon,* and it
would have taken the whole band to kill that many with
stones and clubs. Big Ones' Friend was sitting with
Stonebreaker now, fitting one of the cutting-stones onto
a stick.

This was the fourth night since they had come to this
place. They had slept around a fire at the place where
they had first met Big Ones' Friend. The next morning
Big Ones' Friend had given them the Wonderful Food
of the Big Ones, all he had, a little for each of them. He
had told them that at Wonderful Place the Big Ones
gave it all the time to all Fuzzies, as much as they
wanted. After that, all of them had wanted to go to
Wonderful Place and make friends with the Big Ones,
even Big She. They had wanted to start at once, but Big
Ones' Friend had said that they should build a floating-
thing, a *raft,* and go down the river and over to the
other side. He had said that all the time and work they
put into this would be saved, that it would be far-far to
go up to where this river was little enough to cross without a raft.

Big Ones' Friend had made a little show-like out of
sticks to show the big raft he meant that they should

make. He said the Big Ones often did this, first making something little before making it big to use. Then they had come to this place, and he had said it was a good place to make the raft. So they had made camp, and he had showed them how to make this shelter, and had made a place for their fire, and dug a long hole for the barba-koo fire. Then they had begun digging roots and making rope, and Big Ones' Friend had built fires at the roots of the trees he had wanted for the raft, and burned them till they fell. They cut off the branches with the chopping-stones—*axes*—he and Stonebreaker made out of hard-stone they had found up the little stream, but the trees themselves were too big to cut in that way, so Big Ones' Friend made fires to burn them into logs. This was dangerous; even Big Ones' Friend was afraid about this. These fires might get loose and burn everything. That was why he and Big Ones' Friend would sit up and watch while the others slept, and then they would wake Stabber and Big She and Lame One, who were sleeping now, and after a while they would wake Fruitfinder and Other She and Carries-Bright-Things, and they would watch till daylight.

After a while, Fruitfinder and Carries-Bright-Things and Other She finished the rope they were making and coiled it, and then came into the shelter and lay down to sleep. Stonebreaker worked on at the axehead, and Big Ones' Friend finished putting the one Stonebreaker had made onto a stick. He took it over to the woodpile and tried it while Stonebreaker watched. They both laughed at how good it was. Then he and Stonebreaker came over under the shelter.

"Show shining-stone," Stonebreaker begged.

Big Ones' Friend took it out of his shoulder bag and rubbed it for a while between his hands. Then the three of them leaned together, out of the light of the fire, to look at it. None of them had ever seen a thing like that, but Big Ones' Friend said they were known among Big Ones, and one of his friends, Pappy Vic, dug many of them out of rock. He had found this one while he was breaking a piece of hard black rock he had found up the little stream. It was inside the rock, a stone the shape of a zarabunny's kidney. It looked just like any other stone until it was rubbed; then it shone like a hot coal in the fire. But it was not hot. This was a not-understand thing; even Big Ones' Friend did not know how it could be.

"Pappy Jack used to dig for these stones," Big Ones' Friend said. "Then all the other Big Ones found out about the Fuzzies, and they said Pappy Jack should do nothing but take care of the Fuzzies and teach them."

"Tell more about Pappy Jack. Is he Wise One for all the Big Ones?"

"No. That is Pappy Ben," Big Ones' Friend said. "He is Wise One for Gov'men'. And Pappy Vic is Wise One for Comp'ny; that is another Big One thing, like Gov'men'. Pappy Jack is Wise One for all Fuzzies. All Big Ones listen to Pappy Jack about Fuzzies."

He talked for a long while about Pappy Jack and about Pappy Vic and Pappy Ben and Pappy Gerd and Mummy Woof and Pappy George and the blue-clothes Big Ones, and about Wonderful Place and Big House Place. It was all wonderful, but hard to understand. There were not enough Fuzzy words to tell about every-thing, which was why Big Ones' Friend said they must all learn as many Big One words as they could. They must also learn to make talk from the back of the mouth, so that the Big Ones could hear them. They were practicing that now.

After a while, Stonebreaker became sleepy and lay down. Big Ones' Friend got out his pipe and tobacco and they smoked, taking puffs in turn. One of the night-time sky-lights—*moons* was the Big Ones' word—came up. The Big Ones had names for both of them. This one was called *Zerk-Zees*. The other, which was not in the sky now, was called *Dry-As*. The Big Ones knew all about them; they were very big and very far away, and they went to them in flying things. Big Ones' Friend said he had been on Zerk-Zees, which looked so small, himself. This was hard to believe, but Big Ones' Friend said so.

"You really say for so? You not just make not-so talk?"

Big Ones' Friend was surprised that he should ask a thing like that. "Nobody make not-so talk," he said.

"*I* make not-so talk once." Wise One glad that he could tell something Big Ones' Friend did not know about. "Once I say to others that I see hesh-nazza, damnthing, and was no damnthing."

Then he told how he had wanted to go to find the Big One Place, and the others had wanted to stay where they were.

"So, I tell them I see big damnthing; damnthing chase me. They all frightened. Was no damnthing, but they not know. They all leave place, make run fast up mountain to get away from damnthing. But was no damnthing at all. We go down other side of mountain, not go back."

Big Ones' Friend looked at him in wonder. For all his wisdom, he would not have thought of that. Then he laughed.

"You 'wise one,' " he said. "I not think to do that. But is true I was on Zerk-Zees. Big One take me there to hide when other Big Ones make trouble, once."

He told about Zerk-Zees, but it was hard. He didn't know the words to tell about it. After a while, they both lay down and went to sleep.

It seemed like only a moment, and then Other She was shaking him, crying:

"Wake up, Wise One! Fire burn everything! Big fire!"

He kicked Big Ones' Friend, who was beside him, and sat up. It was so. Everything was brighter than if both moons were biggest and shining together, and there was

a loud noise of crackling and roaring. It was coming
from where they had been burning the trees into logs.
The fire was burning dry things on the ground, and even
small bushes had caught fire. Fruitfinder and Carries-
Bright-Things had branches and were trying to beat it
out, but it was too big and in too many places. Then he
remembered the whistle, and blew it as hard as he could.
By this time, Big Ones' Friend was awake and kicking
Stabber and saying funny Big One words that Wise One
didn't know, and then everybody was awake and all
shouting at the same time.

Stabber caught up his spear and started to run at the
fire with it. Big Ones' Friend caught him by the arm.

"Not kill fire with spear," he said. "Kill fire by take
dry things away from it. Stop, everybody! Not do anything; make think what to do first."

By this time, Carries-Bright-Things and Fruitfinder
came back; Fruitfinder was slapping Carries-Bright-
Things with his hands to put out where her fur had
caught fire, and Carries-Bright-Things was saying,
"Fire too big; not able to kill."

Big Ones' Friend was yelling for everyone to be quiet.
He picked up his axe and went forward a little, then
came back.

"Not put out, too big," he said. "We go where fire
not burn. Fire always burn way wind blow. Fire not
burn on water. We go into water, try to get behind fire.
Then we safe."

"But we go away, fire burn up nice sleeping-place.
Burn up rope. We work hard make rope," somebody
was arguing.

"You want fire burn up *you*?" Wise One asked.
"Then, not make talk. Do what Big Ones' Friend say."
He blew the whistle again, and they were all quiet.
"Now what we do?" he asked Big Ones' Friend.

"Take spears, take axes," Big Ones' Friend said. He
was feeling at his shoulder bag to make sure he had
everything and that it was closed tightly. "Go out in

water as far as can. Wait till fire here burn everything up. Then come out where fire not burn, be safe."

Carries-Bright-Things had gotten the three sticks with the *kata-jes*. She caught Big Ones' Friend by the arm.

"You put in bag, keep safe," she was saying. "Not lose."

She twisted them off the sticks, and Big Ones' Friend put them in his bag. Then he got a long piece of rope and tied one end about his waist.

"Everybody, wrap around waist," he said. "We go in water. Somebody fall in deep place, pull him out."

Nobody had realized that that could be done. Rope was to tie logs together; nobody had thought of using it for anything else. He was called Wise One, and he hadn't even thought of that. By this time, the fire was very big. It had caught a tree that had died from being chewed by goofers and all the branches of it were burning, and another tree next to it had caught fire. All the dry things on the ground were burning along the lake and back away from it, but nothing was burning in the direction from which the wind came toward the fire.

They roped themselves together, everybody carrying a spear and an axe, and went out into the water, until finally it was almost up to their necks. Then they stood still, looking back by the fire. By that time, it had reached the sleeping-place and it had caught fire. The ferns and dry grass blazed up, the brush caught fire, and, as they watched, the pole burned through and everything fell. Some of the band wailed in grief. That had been a good sleeping-place, the best sleeping-place they had ever made. Big Ones' Friend was saying:

"Bloody-hell sunnabish! All good rope, all goofer skins, all logs, all burn up. Now have to do again."

They waited a long time in the water. It grew hot even where they were. They had to take deep breaths and draw their heads down under the water for as long as they could and then raise them to breathe again. The air was hot and full of smoke, and bits of burning things fell among them. Whole trees were burning now. Different kinds of trees burned in different ways. Longleaf trees caught fire quickly, and then the leaves all burned and the fire went out, and then the branches would catch fire in places. But the blue roundleaf trees would not catch at first, but then they would catch all over and great flames would shoot high.

Finally, the fire close to them grew less, though the big trees were all burning. It had burned far away in the direction the wind blew. Big Ones' Friend said that the ground would be hot where the fire had been, and burn their feet, so they waded along where the water was shallow to where the small moving-water came into the lake. The fire had started to burn along this, but not across it, so they crossed over and started up on the other side. Big Ones' Friend untied the rope from around his waist, and they wrapped it around the staff of a spear; Big She and Lame One carried it.

Animals were in the woods, all frightened by the fire. They came close enough to a takku, a zarabuck, to kill it with their spears. But why should they? They would only have to carry the meat with them, and it might be that they would have to run fast to get away from the fire. The little stream turned and came from the direction the fire was burning. Then they came to a place where there was fire on their side too. Everybody was frightened because Big Ones' Friend had said that fire would not cross a moving-water, but he could see how this had happened: the wind had carried little burning-things over it, and started new fires.

"We go away from here," Big Ones' Friend said. "Soon be fire all around. Go away through woods; keep wind in face."

Everybody began to run. The brush was thick. After a while, Wise One saw Lame One running alone with his spear and axe, and then he saw Big She with only an axe. Big Ones' Friend would be angry with them; they had thrown away the spear on which the rope was wrapped. The brush became more thick, and now there were also long vines. These vines would be good to tie logs together for a raft. He would try to remember them when they came to build a new raft. He was going to speak of it to Big Ones' Friend, but when they stopped to catch their breath, Big Ones' Friend was saying the funny mean-nothing Big One words. Maybe he was frightened. This was a bad place to be, with the fire so near.

At first the moon, Zerk-Zees, which was more than half round, was on their left as they ran, and a little in front. After a while, he saw that it was almost directly in front of them, though it was only a little higher. He spoke of this to Big Ones' Friend and also to Stabber. They stopped, and Big Ones' Friend got out his point-north thing, and made a light with his firemaker. Then he said more Big One words.

"Wind change. Maybe change more, maybe bring fire to us. Come, make run fast."

They floundered on through the brush and among the vines and trees. After a while they came to a big moving-water, not as big as the one that made wide lake-places, but still big. They could not cross. There was argument about what to do. The fire was up the river, but if they went down they would come to where it came into the lake, and that would be a bad place to get out of. He looked in the direction of the fire and was glad that he could not see yellow flames, though all the sky was bright pink. The wind still blew toward the fire, so they decided to go down the river.

The brush became less thick, and here were tall long-leaf trees. There were animals all about, moving in the woods, frightened by the fire. Then, ahead they saw the light of Zerk-Zees shining on the lake.

"Not go that way," somebody—Wise One thought it was Stonebreaker—said.

"Not go across moving-water either," Big She said. "Too deep."

"Make raft," Big Ones' Friend said. "Little raft. Get big sticks, tie together with rope, put things on. Some get on raft, some swim. Who has rope?"

Nobody had the rope. Lame One and Big She had thrown it away to run faster. Big Ones' Friend said one of the mean-nothing words, then thought for a moment. "We go along lake, that way." He pointed east, where the thin edge of Dry-As was just above the horizon. "Go back to place fire start. Maybe all dead, ground cool. Then we be safe."

Fruitfinder said he was hungry. Now that it was said, everybody else was hungry too. They found a goofer, so frightened that Stabber just walked up to it and speared it. Big Ones' Friend took out his knife, skinned it, and cut it up. They did not make a fire to cook it. Nobody, not even Big Ones' Friend, wanted to make fire here, and they did not want to wait while it cooked. They all ate it raw.

While they were eating he smelled smoke, but thought it was an old smell in his fur. Then Carries-Bright-Things said she smelled smoke, and so did Stone-breaker. They stopped eating and looked about. The fire was much brighter, and they could see yellow flames among the red-pink glow over the trees.

Big Ones' Friend said, "Jeeze-krise go-hell bloody damn! Wind change again. Fire that way, wind come from fire, bring fire here!"

xxi.

Jack Holloway was bringing a hangover home from Mallorysport, but even without it he'd have felt like Nifflheim. Traveling east was always a bother—three hours air-time and three hours zone-difference. You had to get up before daylight to get in by cocktail-time. He winced at the thought of cocktails; right now he'd as soon drink straight rat poison.

He'd done too much drinking since—since Little Fuzzy got drowned, go ahead and say it—and it hadn't done a damn's worth of good; as soon as he sobered up, he felt worse about it than ever. Hell, he'd had friends killed before, on Thor and Loki and Shesha and Mimir. Everywhere but on Terra; people didn't get killed on Terra anymore, they just dropped dead on golf courses. If it had been anybody but Little Fuzzy . . . Why, Little Fuzzy was just about the most important person in the universe to him.

His head thumped and throbbed as though an over-powered and badly defective engine were running inside it. Too many cocktails before dinner at Government House when he got in, and then too many drinks in the evening with all that crowd after dinner. And the cocktail party after the opening of the Fuzzy Club; he'd needed a lot of liquor to keep from thinking how much Little Fuzzy would have enjoyed that.

They were going to put in a big commemorative
plaque for Little Fuzzy, eight feet by ten: Little Fuzzy in
gold with a silver chopper-digger on a dark bronze
ground. He'd seen the sketches for it. It was going to be
beautiful when it was done, looked just like the little
fellow.

And then, when he'd wanted to go home, Ben and
Gus had insisted that he stay over for the banquet for
the delegates, and he wanted to help get them in a good
humor. And, God, what a gang! One thing, they were
all in favor of lynching Hugo Ingermann.

George Lunt, beside him, had tried to make conversa-
tion after they'd lifted out, then gave it up. He'd tried to
sleep, and must have dozed off in his seat a few times.
Each time he woke, his head hurt worse and he had
a fouler taste in his mouth. He was awake when they
passed over Big Blackwater; not a sign of smoke or anything going on. Grego'd moved everything he had there
up to Yellowsand and was bringing men and equipment
in from Alpha and Delta and Gamma. He'd seen one of
the Company's big contragravity freighters, the *Zebralope*, lifting out of Mallorysport air terminal for Yellowsand when he was leaving Government House. He
hoped Grego got out a lot of sunstones before the trial.

Coming up Cold Creek, he couldn't see any activity
where they'd been holding the raft-building classes.
There weren't many Fuzzies running around the camp
either, though there was a small archery class. Gerd van
Riebeek met him and shook hands with him as he got
out. George Lunt excused himself and went off toward
the ZNPF Headquarters. He'd have to look at his desk;
he hated the thought of having to deal with what would
be piled up on it.

Gerd was silly enough to ask him how he was.

"I have a hangover with little hangovers, and some of
the little ones are just before having young. Is there any
hot coffee around?"

That was a silly question, too; this was an office, and

offices ran on hot coffee. They went into his office; Gerd called for some to be brought in. There was a stack of papers half the size of a cotton bale—he'd been right about that. He hung up his hat and they sat down.

"Didn't see much of a crowd outside," he mentioned.

"A hundred and fifty less," Gerd told him. "They're down in the Squiggle."

"Good God!" He knew what the Squiggle was like. "What are a hundred and fifty of our Fuzzies doing in that place?"

Gerd grinned. "Working for the CZC, like everybody else. They're shooting goofers with bows and arrows. Company had a lot of goofers in those young feather-leaf trees they planted the watersheds with. Three days ago I sent fifty down to the chief forester at Chesterville. By yesterday morning they'd shot over two hundred goofers, so he wanted a hundred more, and I sent them. Captain Knabber and five Protection Force troopers are with them; Pancho went down with the second draft to observe. They're dropping them off in squads of half a dozen, supplying and transporting them with air-lorries. In the evenings, they bring them into a couple of camps they've set up."

"Why, I'll be damned!" In spite of the headache, which the coffee was barely beginning to ameliorate, Jack chuckled. "Bet they're having a great time. Your idea?"

"Yes. Juan Jimenez told me about the goofer situation. I'd been bothered about possible side effects of exterminating the harpies. The harpies kept the goofer increase down to reasonable limits, and now there are no harpies down there. I thought Fuzzies would do the job just as well. It's axiomatic that a man with a rifle is the most efficient predator. Fuzzies with bows and arrows seem to be almost as good."

"We'll have rifles for them before long. Mart Burgess finished the ones for Gus's Allan and Natty—I wish I could shoot like those Fuzzies!—and he's making up a couple more for prototypes and shop-models for the Company. They're going to produce them in quantity."

"What kind of rifles? Safe for Fuzzies to use?"

"Yes, single-shots. Burgess got the action design from an old book. Remington rolling-block; they used them all over Terra in the first century Pre-Atomic."

"That might be an answer to what you're worrying about, Jack," Gerd said. "You want something the Fuzzies can do to earn what they get from us, so they won't turn into bums. Pest-control hunters."

That idea of Fuzzy colonies on other continents . . . There was a burrowing rodent on Gamma that was driving the farmers crazy. And land-prawns everywhere; they were distributed all over the planet. And Fuzzies loved to hunt.

The harpies had been exterminated completely on Delta Continent. There'd be something there that they had fed on, which would now be proliferating and turning destructive. Jack had some more coffee brought in, and he and Gerd talked about that for a while. Then Gerd went out, and he talked to the Company forester at Chesterville by screen, and to Pancho Ybarra, whom he located at one of the temporary Fuzzy hunting-camps. Then he started on the accumulation of paperwork.

He was still at it when the screen buzzed; one of the girls at message center.

"Mr. Holloway, we've just gotten a call from Yellow-sand Canyon," she began.

A clutching tightness in his chest. A call from Yellow-sand might just be some routine matter, but then again, it might be . . . He forced calmness into his voice.

"Yes?"

"Well, the *Zebralope*, coming in from Mallorysport, reported sighting a big forest-fire up Lake-Chain River. They've transmitted in some views they took, and Mr. McGinnis, the Company general superintendent, sent a survey boat out to look at it. He thought you ought to be notified, since it's on the Fuzzy Reservation. He's calling Mr. Grego now for instructions.''

"Just where is it?"

She gave him the map coordinates. He jotted them down and told her to stand by. He snapped on a reading-screen, twisted the class-selector for maps, and then fiddled to get the latest revised map of the country up the Lake-Chain, finally centering the cross hairs on the given coordinates and stepping up magnification.

Funny place for a forest-fire, he thought. There hadn't been any thunderstorms up that way for ten days. Not since the night Little Fuzzy was lost. Of course, a fire could smoulder for ten days, but . . .

"Let's have the views," he said.

"Just a moment, sir."

A lot of things could start fires in the woods, but they were all hundred-to-one shots but two: Lightning and carelessness. Carelessness of some human—sapient, he corrected—being. And the commonest sort of carelessness was careless smoking. Little Fuzzy smoked; he'd had his pipe and tobacco and lighter with him in his shoulder bag.

There'd been a lot of trees and stuff uprooted above that had been shoved down into the canyon. Suppose he'd managed to grab hold of something and kept himself afloat; and suppose he'd managed to get out of the river . . .

He reduced magnification and widened the field. Yes. Suppose he'd been carried down below the mouth of the Lake-Chain River, on the left bank. He'd start back on foot, and when he came to where the Lake-Chain came in from the north to join the Yellowsand curving in from the east, what would he think?

Well, what would anybody who didn't know the country think? He'd think the Lake-Chain was the Yellowsand, and go on following it. Of course, he had a compass, but he wouldn't be looking at that, hanging to a log or a tree in the river. A compass would only tell him which way north was; it wouldn't tell him where he'd been since he last looked at it.

"I have the fire views now, Mr. Holloway."

"Don't bother with them. I'll get them later. You call Gerd van Riebeek and George Lunt; tell them I want them right away. And tell Lunt to put on an emergency alert. And then get me Victor Grego in Mallorysport."

He reached for his pipe and lighter, wondering where his hangover had gone.

"And when you have time," he added, "call Sandra Glenn at the Fuzzy Club in Mallorysport and tell her to hold up work on that commemorative plaque. It might just be a little premature."

xxii.

Little Fuzzy's eyes smarted, his throat was sore and his mouth dry. His fur was singed. There was one place on his back where he had been burned painfully, and would have been burned worse if someone behind had not slapped out the fire. He was filthy, caked with mud and blackened with soot. They all were. They had just gotten out of mud and were standing on the bank of the small stream, looking about them.

There was nothing green anywhere they looked, nothing but black, dusted with gray ash and wreathed in gray smoke that rose from things that still burned. Many trees still stood, but they were all black with smoke and little tongues of flame blowing from them. The sun had come out, but it was hard to see, dim and red, through the smoke that rose everywhere.

They stood in a little clump beside the stream. No one spoke. Lame One was really lame now; he had burned his foot and limped in pain, leaning on a spear. Wise One had been hurt too, by a broken branch that had bounced and hit him when a tree had fallen nearby. There was dried blood in his fur along with the mud and soot. Most of the others had been cut and scratched in the brush or bruised by falls, but not badly. They had lost most of their things.

Little Fuzzy still had his shoulder bag and his knife

and trowel and his axe. Wise One had an axe, and he
still had the whistle. Big She had an axe, and so did
Stonebreaker. Stabber had a spear, as did Lame One
and Other She. All the other weapons had been lost
swimming the river that flowed into the lake after the
wind had turned and brought the fire toward them.

"Now what do?" Stabber was asking. "Not go back,
big fire that way. Big fire that way too." He pointed up
the stream. "And not go where fire was, ground hot, all
burn feet like Lame One."

He had always wondered why Big Ones wore the
hard, stiff things on their feet. Now he knew; they could
walk anywhere with them. A Big One could walk over
the ground here that was still smoking. He wished now
that they had carried away the skins of the goofers and
zarabunnies they had killed; but of course, if they had
they would have lost them in the water too.

"Big Ones' Friend know about fire," Stonebreaker
said. "We not know. Big Ones' Friend tell us what to
do."

He didn't know what to do either. He would have to
think and remember everything Pappy Jack and Pappy
Gerd and Pappy George and the others had told him,
and everything he had seen and learned since this fire
had begun.

Fire would not live where there was nothing to burn,
or in water, or ground. It would not burn wet things,
but it would make wet things dry, and then they would
burn. That was not the fire itself, but the heat of the
fire. He didn't understand about that, because heat was
not a thing but just the way things were. Pappy Jack
had told him that. He still didn't quite understand, but
he knew fire made heat.

Fire couldn't live without air. He wasn't sure just
what air was, but it was everywhere, and when it moved
it made wind. Fire burned in the way the wind blew; this
was so, but he had seen fire burning, very little and very
slow, against the wind. But the big part of the fire went

with the wind; that was what had made the bad trouble last night, when the wind had changed.

And fire always burned up; he had seen that happen at the beginning when the little dry things on the ground caught fire and the fire went up into the trees and burned them. He could still see it burning up the trees that were standing. There were two kinds of woods fires, and he had seen both kinds. One kind burned on the ground, among the bushes, and set fire to the trees above it. That had been how this fire had started. Then there were fires that got into the tops of trees and lit one treetop from another. Little burning things fell down and set fire to what was on the ground, and this burned after the big fire in the treetops. This was a bad kind of fire; with a strong wind it moved very fast. Nobody could escape by running ahead of it.

"Big Ones' Friend not say anything," Big She objected.

"Big Ones' Friend make think," Wise One said. "Not think, do wrong thing. Do wrong thing, all make dead."

Maybe it would be best just to stay here all day and wait for the ground to get cool and the little burning things to go out. He thought that the place where they had camped and where the fire had started was to the east of them, but he wasn't sure. There was a lake to the south of them, he knew that, but he didn't know which one. There were too many lakes in this place. And there were too many bloody-hell sunnabish fires all around!

"Nothing to eat, this place," Carries-Bright-Things complained. "Good-to-eat things all burn."

As soon as she said that, everybody remembered that they were hungry. They had eaten a goofer, but that had been a long time ago, and they had not been able to finish it.

"We have to find not-burn-yet place, then find good-to-eat things." The trouble was, he didn't know where there were any not-burn-yet places, and if they found

one maybe the fire would come and then there would be
more trouble. He looked up the stream. "I think we go
that way. Maybe find not-burn place, maybe find place
where fire all dead, ground cool."

And then they would have to get back to the lakes and
find a place to camp and start building a raft. He
thought of all the work they had done that they would
have to do over, the rope they would have to make, the
things to work with, the logs. That was a sick-making
thing to think of. And the trouble he and Wise One and
Stabber would have with some of the others. . . .

They started up the stream, with the whole country
burned black, gray with smoke and ashes on either side,
and the black trees standing, still burning. They waded
where the water was not too deep. Where it was, they
walked on the bank, careful to avoid burning things.
The stream bent; now they were going straight west.

Then they heard an aircar sound. They all stopped
and listened. Pappy Jack had always told him that if he
were lost, he should build a fire and make a big smoke,
so that somebody would see. He had to laugh at that.
This time he had made a big smoke. Some Big One, even
far away, had seen it and come to see what made it.
Then he was disappointed. He knew what the sound
was. It was not an aircar nearby but a big air-thing, a
ship, far off. He knew about them. One came every
three days to Wonderful Place, bringing things. It was
always fun when a ship came; none of the Fuzzies would
stay in school but would all run out to watch.

He wondered why a ship was in this place, and then
he thought that it would be coming to Yellowsand,
bringing more machines and more of Pappy Vic's
friends to help him dig, and things to eat, and *likka* for
koktel-drinko, and everything the Big Ones needed. The
Big Ones on the ship would see the smoke and tell
Pappy Vic, and then Pappy Vic and his friends would
come.

The only trouble was, this fire was too big. It was

burning everywhere. Why, it would take a person days
to walk all around where it had burned. How would the
Big Ones know where to look, and from the air, how
could they see for all this smoke? Pappy Jack had said,
make smoke. Well, he had made too much smoke. If it
had not been so dreadful, that would have been a laugh-
at thing.

He mustn't let the others think about this, though.
So, as they waded up the little stream, he talked to them
about Wonderful Place, of the estee-fee they ate, and
the milk and fruit juice, and the school where the Big
Ones taught new things nobody had ever thought about,
and the bows and arrows, and the hard stuff that they
heated to make soft and pounded into any shape they
wanted and then made hard again, and the marks that
meant sounds, so that when one looked at them one
could say the words somebody else had said when making them. He told them how many Fuzzies there were at
Wonderful Place, and all the fun they had. He told
them about how all Fuzzies would have nice Big Ones of
their own, to take care of them and be good to them. It
made a good-feeling just to talk about these things.

Then, through the smoke ahead, he saw green, and
then all the others saw it and shouted and ran forward,
even Lame One hobbling on his spear. The fire had
stopped at a little stream that flowed into this one from
the south, and beyond was green grass and bushes. But
there were old black trees here, burned and dead, with
moss on them. The others, all but Wise One, could not
understand this.

"Long-ago big burn-everything fire," Wise One said.
"Maybe lightning make. Burn everything here, same
like that." He pointed to the smoking burn-place behind. "Then grass grow, bushes grow, but this fire not
find anything to burn."

They crossed into the long-ago-burned place. The
ground was still black, although the other fire had been
many new-leaf times ago. Here he cut the tallest and

straightest of the bushes, making a staff for Lame One so that Carries-Bright-Things could take his spear, and he made a club for Fruitfinder. Then they made line-abreast and went forward, and almost at once they killed a zarabunny, and then a goofer. . . .

Using his trowel, he dug a trench, and they built a fire in it and sat down and watched the meat cooking on sticks over it. He and Big She took the zarabunny skin and put it around Lame One's hurt foot and cut strips from the goofer skin to fasten it on. Lame One got up and limped about to try it and said that it did not hurt him so much to walk. After they ate he filled his pipe and lit it, and those who liked to smoke passed it around.

He was very careful to bury all the fire before they left. Everybody thought it was funny that they were making a fire with fire all around them.

There was smoke ahead, but the wind was at their backs. Soon the burned-dead trees became less, and then there were white dead trees, with all their branches. He thought that these trees had made dead because the bark had been burned at the bottoms, just as trees were killed by goofers chewing the bark. The brush was more and bigger here. And finally they came to big round-blue-leaf trees that had not been burned at all. The fire had never been here.

Nobody wanted to go fast. It was nice among the big trees, and the smoke in the air was less, though they could still smell it and it made the sun dim. They found a little stream, clear and sweet, untainted by ashes. They drank and washed all the mud and soot out of their fur. Everybody felt much better.

He began hearing aircar sounds again, very far away, but many of them, and also machinery sounds. Pappy Vic and his friends must have come and brought machines to help them put out the fire. He remembered all the things he had seen at Yellowsand, how they were digging off the whole top of the mountain. They would have no trouble putting out a fire even as big as this one. He wanted to go in the direction of the sounds, but he knew that the fire was between.

The ground sloped up, but his compass told him that they were still going south; it seemed to him that the land should slope down in that direction. Then they came to the top of a hill. When they went forward they could see a lake ahead and below, a very wide lake. They stopped at the edge of a cliff, higher than the highest house in Wonderful Place, as high as the middle terrace of Pappy Ben's house in Big House Place, and right at the bottom with no beach at all was the lake.

"Not go down there," Lame One said. "Not even if foot not hurt. Too far, nothing to hold to, not climb."

"Go down, get in water," Stabber said.

"Water deep down there. Always deep, place like that," Wise One added.

Other She looked apprehensively at the great round clouds of smoke rising to the north.

"Maybe fire come this way. Maybe this not good place."

He was beginning to think so himself. The fire had stopped at the long-ago-burned place, but he didn't know what it was doing at the other side. Still, he didn't want to leave this place. It was high, and the trees were not too many. If somebody came over the lake in an air-car, they could see and come for them. He said so.

"Why not come now?" Other She asked. "Not see Big One flying things anywhere."

"Not know we here. All work hard put out fire. Is always-so thing with Big Ones; hear about fire in woods, go with machines to put out."

He opened his pouch to see how much tobacco he had left. He had been careful not to waste it, but it had been two hands, *ten*, days ago since he fell in the river. There was only a little, but he filled the pipe and lit it, passing

it around. Stabber, who hadn't liked it before, thought
he would try it again. He coughed on the first puff, but
after that he said he liked it.

When there was nothing left in the pipe but ashes, he
put it away, and then looked to the north. There was
much more smoke, and it was closer. The sound of the
fire could be heard now, and once he thought he could
see it over the tops of the trees. The others were becoming frightened.

"Where go?" Fruitfinder was almost wailing. "Is far
down, water close, water deep." He pointed to the east.
"And more fire there. We not go anywhere fire not be."

He was afraid Fruitfinder was right, but that was not
a good way to talk. Soon everyone would be frightened,
and frightened people did foolish things. Being frightened was a good way to make dead. He looked to the
east where the cliff ended in a promontory that jutted
out into the lake. It was hard to tell; far-off things
always looked little, but he thought it was less high
there. For one thing, smoke was blowing past it out over
the lake.

"Not so far down that way," he said. "Maybe can
get down to water; fire not come down."

Nobody else knew what to do, so nobody argued. To
the north, he could now see much fire above the trees.
Krisa-mitee, he thought, now makes sunnabish treetop
fire; this is bad! They all hurried along the top of the
cliff, near the edge. Once they came to a place where a
piece of the cliff had slid down into the lake; it looked
like the place where Pappy Vic's friends had been digging at Yellowsand, where they had found no shining
stones and stopped, and where he had gone down into
the deep place. They all ran around it and kept on. By
this time the fire was close; it was a treetop fire, and
burning things were falling and making fires under it on
the ground.

He thought, Maybe this is where Little Fuzzy make
dead!

He didn't want to die. He wanted to go back to Pappy Jack.

Then he stopped short. He was sure of it. This was where Little Fuzzy and Wise One and Stabber and Lame One and Fruitfinder and Stonebreaker and Big She and Other She and Carries-Bright-Things would all make dead.

In front of them was a deep-down split in the ground, down as far as the cliff itself, and at the bottom of it a stream rushed out into the lake, fast and foam-white. He looked to the left; it went as far as he could see. Behind, the fire roared toward them. It seemed to be making its own wind; he didn't know fire could do that. Bits of flaming stuff were being swirled high into the air; some were falling halfway to them from the fire and starting little fires for themselves.

xxiii.

The smoke of the fire wasn't visible at all when Jack Holloway came in. Yellowsand looked quiet from the air, the diggings empty of equipment and deserted. Every machine must have been shifted north and west to the fire. He saw a few people around the fenced-in flint-cracking area, mostly in CZC Police uniform. The *Zebralope* was gone, probably sent off for reinforcements. He set the car down in front of the administration hut, and half a dozen men advanced to meet him. Luther McGinnis, the superintendent; Stan Farr, the personnel man; José Durrante, the forester; Harry Steefer. He and Gerd got out; the two ZNPF troopers in the front seat followed them.

"We have Mr. Grego on screen now," McGinnis said. "He's in his yacht, about halfway from Alpha; he has a load of fire-fighting experts with him. You know what he thinks?"

"The same as I do; I was talking to him. Little Fuzzy got careless dumping out his pipe. I have to watch that myself, and I've been smoking in the woods longer than he has."

Gerd was asking just where the fire was.

"Show you," McGinnis said. "But if you think it really was Little Fuzzy, how in Nifflheim did he get away up there?"

"Walked." Jack gave his reasons for thinking so while they were going toward the hut door. "He probably thought he was going up the Yellowsand till he got up to the lakes."

There was a monster military-type screen rigged inside, fifteen feet square; in it a view of the fire, from around five thousand feet, rotated slowly as the vehicle on which the pickup was mounted circled over it. He'd seen a lot of forest-fires, helped fight most of them. This one was a real baddie, and if it hadn't been for the big river and the lakes that clustered along it like variously shaped leaves on a vine, it would have been worse. It was all on the north side, and from the way the smoke was blowing, the water-barriers had it stopped.

"Wind must have done a lot of shifting," he commented.

"Yes." That was the camp meteorologist. "It was steady from the southwest last night; we think the fire started sometime after midnight. A little before daybreak, it started moving around, blowing more toward the north, and then it backed around to the southwest where it had come from. That was general wind, of course. In broken country like that, there are always a lot of erratic ground winds. After the fire started, there were convection currents from the heat."

"Never can trust the wind in a fire," he said.

"Hey, Jack! Is that you?" a voice called. "You just get in?"

He turned in the direction of the speaker whence it came, saw Victor Grego in bush-clothes in one of the communication-screens, with a background that looked like an air-yacht cabin.

"Yes. I'm going out and have a look as soon as I find out where. I have a couple more cars on the way, George Lunt and some ZNPF, and three lorries full of troopers and construction men following. I didn't bring any equipment. All we have is light stuff, and it'd take four or five hours to get it here on its own contragravity."

Grego nodded. "We have plenty of that. I'll be getting in around 1430; I probably won't see you till you get back in. I hope the kid did start it, and I hope I didn't get caught in it afterward."

So did Jack. Be a hell of a note, getting out of Yellowsand River alive and then getting burned in this fire. No, Little Fuzzy was too smart to get caught.

He looked at other screens, views transmitted in from vehicles over the fire-lines—bulldozers flopping off contragravity in the woods and snorting forward, sending trees toppling in front of them; manipulators picking them up as they fell and carrying them away; draglines and scoops dumping earth and rock to windward. People must have been awfully helpless with a big fire before they had contragravity. They'd only gotten onto this around noon, and they'd have it all out by sunset; he'd read about old-time forest-fires that had burned for days.

"These people all been warned to keep an eye out for a Fuzzy running around?" he asked McGinnis.

"Yes, that's gone out to everybody. I hope he's alive and out of danger. We'll have a Nifflheim of a time finding him after the fire's out, though."

"You may have a Nifflheim of a time putting out the next fire he starts. He may have started this one for a smoke signal." He turned to Durrante. "How much do you know about that country up there?"

"Well, I've been out with survey crews all over it." That meant, at a couple of thousand feet. "I know what's in there."

"Okay. Gerd and I are going out now. Suppose you come along. Where do you think this started?"

"I'll show you." Durrante led them to a table map, now marked in different shadings of red. "As nearly as I can figure, in about here, along the north shore of this

lake. The first burn was along the shore and up this run;
that was while the wind was still blowing northeast. It
was burning all over here, and here, when the *Zebralope*
sighted it, but that was after the wind shifted. We didn't
get a car to the scene till around 1030, and by that time
this area was burned out, nothing but snags burning,
and there was a hell of a crown-fire going over this way.
This part here is an old burn, fire started by lightning
maybe fifteen years ago. There was nobody on this continent north of the Big Bend then. The fire hasn't gotten
in there at all. This hill is all in bluegums; that's where
the latest crown-fire's going."

"Okay. Let's go."

They went out to the car. Gerd took the controls; the
forester got in beside him. Jack took the back seat,
where he could look out on both sides.

"Hand my rifle back to me," he said. "I'll want it if I
get out to look around on foot."

The forester lifted it out of the clips on the dash-
board; it was the 12.7-mm double. "Good Lord, you
lug a lot of gun around," he said, passing it back.

"I may have a lot of animal to stop. You run into a
damnthing at ten yards, seven thousand foot-pounds
isn't too much."

"N-no," Durrante agreed. "I never used anything
heavier than a 7-mm, myself." He never bothered with
a rifle at a fire; animals, he said, never attacked when
running away from a fire.

Now, there was the kind of guy they make angels out
of. That was all he knew about damnthings; a scared
damnthing would attack anything that moved, just because it was scared. Some human people were like that
too.

They came in over the lakes a trifle above the point
where the fire was supposed to have started and let
down on the black and ash-powdered shore. A lot of
snags, some large, were still burning. They were damn
good things to stay away from. He saw one sway and

fall in a cloud of pink spark, powdered dust, and smoke. He climbed out of the car, broke the double express, and slipped in two of the thumb-thick, span-long cartridges, snapping it shut and checking the safety. Wouldn't be anything alive here, but he hadn't lived to be past seventy by taking things for granted. Durrante, who got out with him, had only a pistol. If he stayed on Beta, maybe he wouldn't get to be that old.

It was Durrante who spotted the little triangle of unburned grass between the mouth of the run and the lake. At the apex a tree had been burned off at the base and the branches lopped off with something that had made not quite rectilinear cuts—a little flint hatchet, maybe. The fire had started on both sides of it, eight feet from the butt. He let out his breath in a whoosh of relief. Up to this, he had only hoped Little Fuzzy had gotten out of the river alive and started the fire; now he *knew* it.

"He wasn't trying to make a signal-fire," he said. "He was building himself a raft." He looked at the log. "How the devil did he expect to get that into the water, though? It'd take half a dozen Fuzzies to roll that."

Under a couple of blackened and still burning snags he found what was left of Little Fuzzy's camp, burned branches mixed with the powdery ash of grass and fern-fronds; a pile of ash that showed traces of having been coils of rope made from hair-roots. He found bones which frightened him until he saw that they were all goofer and zarabunny bones. Little Fuzzy hadn't gone hungry. Durrante found a lot of flint, broken and chipped, a flint spearhead and an axehead, and, among some tree-branch ashes, another axehead with fine beryl-steel wire around it and the charred remains of an axe-helve.

"Little Fuzzy was here, all right. He always carried a spool of wire around with him." He slung his rifle and got out his pipe and tobacco. Gerd had brought the car to within a yard of the ground and had his head out the open window beside him. He handed the remains of the axe up to him. "What do you think, Gerd?"

"If you were a Fuzzy and you woke up in the middle of the night with the woods on fire, what would you do?" Gerd asked.

"Little Fuzzy knows a few of the simpler principles of thermodynamics. I think he'd get out in the water as far as he could and sit tight till the fire was past, and then try to get to windward of it. Let's go up along the lake shore first."

Gerd set the car down and they got in. Jack didn't bother unloading the big rifle. West of the little run, the whole country was burned, but that must have happened after the wind backed around. The lake narrowed into the river; the river twisted and widened into another lake, with a ground-fire going furiously on the left bank. Then they came to a promontory jutting into the water a couple of hundred feet high. On top of it a crown-fire was just before burning out, with a ground-fire raging behind it. They passed a narrow gorge, just a split in the cliff, with a stream tumbling out of it. Things were burning on both sides of it on the top.

He had the window down and was peering out; a little beyond the gorge he heard the bellowing of some big animal in agony—something the fire had caught and hadn't quite killed. He shoved the muzzle of the 12.7-double out the window.

"See if you can see where it is, Gerd. Whatever it is, we don't want to leave it like that."

"I see it," Gerd said, a moment later. "Over where that chunk slid out of the cliff."

Then he saw it. It was a damnthing, a monster, with a brow-horn long enough to make a walking stick and side-horns as big as sickles. It had blundered into a hollow, burned and probably blinded, and fallen, until its body caught on a point of rock. The sounds it was making were like nothing he had ever heard a damnthing make before; it was a frightful pain.

Kneeling on the floor, he closed his sights on the beast's head just below an ear that was now a lump of undercooked meat, and squeezed. He'd been a little off balance; the recoil almost knocked him over. When he looked again, the damnthing was still.

"Move in a little, Gerd. Back a bit." He wanted to be sure, and with a damnthing the only way to be sure was shoot it again. "I think it's dead, but . . ."

Somewhere a whistle blew shrilly, then blew again and again.

"What the hell?" Gerd was asking.

"Why, it's in the middle of that fire!" Durrante cried. "Nothing could live in there."

Wanting to get as much for his cartridge and his pounded shoulder as he could, he aimed at the damnthing's head and let off the left barrel with another thunderclap report. The body jerked from the impact of the bullet and nothing else.

"It's up that gorge. I told you Little Fuzzy knows a few of the rudiments of thermodynamics. He's down under the head, sitting it out. You think you can get the car in there?"

"I can get her in. I'll probably have to get her out straight up, though, through the fire, so have everything shut when I do."

They inched into the gorge. Twenty-feet width would have been plenty, if it had been straight. It wasn't, and there were times when it looked like a no-go. Ahead, the whistle was still blowing, and he could hear calls of "Pappy Jack! Pappy Jack!" in several voices, he realized, while the whistle was blowing. And there was yeeking. Little Fuzzy had picked up a gang; that was how he was going to get that log into the water.

"Hang on, Little Fuzzy!" he shouted. "Pappy Jack come!"

There was a nasty scraping as Gerd got the patrol car around a corner. Then he saw them. Nine of them, by golly. Little Fuzzy, still wearing his shoulder bag, and eight others. One had a foot bandaged in what looked like a zarabunny skin. A couple had flint-tipped spears and flint axes, the heads bound on with wire. They were all clinging to an out-thrust ledge, halfway down to the water.

Gerd got the car down. Jack opened the door and reached out, pulling the nearest Fuzzy into the car. It was a female, with an axe. She clung to it as he got her into the car. He picked up the one with the bandaged foot and got him in, handing him forward and warning Durrante to be careful of the foot. Little Fuzzy was next; he was saying, "Pappy Jack! You *did* come!" and then, "And Pappy Gerd!" Then he shouted encouragement to the others outside until they were all in the car.

"Now, we all go to Wonderful Place," Little Fuzzy was saying. "Pappy Jack take care of us. Pappy Jack friend of all Fuzzies. You see what I tell."

He saw Grego's maroon and silver air-yacht grounded by the administration hut as they came in. Gerd, in front, had already called in the rescue of Little Fuzzy and eight other assorted Fuzzies. There was a crowd; he saw Grego and Diamond in front. Gerd set down the car and Durrante got out carrying the burned-foot case. He opened the rear door and waited for the other survivors to pile out under their own power. Those who could speak audibly—Little Fuzzy seemed to have been teaching them to talk like Big Ones—wanted to know if this place Hoksu-Mitto. They were given an ovation, Diamond rushing forward as soon as he saw his friend. Then they were all herded into the camp hospital.

Little Fuzzy had a burn on his back and a lot of fur singed off. He was treated first, to show the others that they would be medicated instead of murdered. The burned foot was really nasty, especially as the Fuzzy had been walking on it quite a lot. Everybody praised the zarabunny-skin wrapping. The camp doctor wanted to put the lot of them to bed. He didn't know enough about Fuzzies to know that no Fuzzy with anything less than a broken leg could be kept in bed. As soon as they were all bandaged up, they were taken to the executives' living quarters for an Extee Three banquet, and when that was over, they all wanted *smokko*.

The news services began screening in almost at once, wanting views and interviews. They weren't much interested in the fire; they wanted Little Fuzzy and his new friends. It was a pain in the neck, but Grego insisted that they be fully satisfied; with the Constitutional Convention just opened, the Friends of Little Fuzzy needed a good press. It was well after dinner-time, and the fire had been stopped all around its perimeter, before anybody could get any privacy at all.

The Fuzzies were sprawled on a couple of mattresses on the floor, all but Little Fuzzy who wanted to sit on Pappy Vic. It was taking a long time for Little Fuzzy to tell about everything that had happened since he'd gone in the river in Yellowsand Canyon; apparently he had already told the other Fuzzies his adventures, because they were constantly interrupting to remind him of things he was forgetting. Then, after he got to where he had joined Wise One and his band—Wise One was the one who had the whistle and the bandaged head—everybody tried to tell about it at once. Harry Steefer and José Durrante were missing a lot of it because they couldn't understand Fuzzy. It was surprising how well this crowd had learned to pitch their voices to human audibility in the time Little Fuzzy had been with them.

Finally, Little Fuzzy got to where, trying to run ahead of the crown-fire at the top of the cliff, they had found themselves stopped by the deep chasm.

"Come this place, not get over, we think all make dead," Little Fuzzy said. "Then I remember what

Pappy Jack say. Fire make heat, heat always go up,
never go down. So we go down, heat go away from us.
Then Pappy Jack come."

That called for praise, which Little Fuzzy accepted as
his due, with becoming modesty.

"Pappy Jack smart, too. Not make shoot with big
rifle, we not hear, not blow whistle."

Let it go at that; hell, he couldn't have gone on and
left that damnthing bellowing in pain. He wanted to
know how Wise One and his band had first learned
about the Big Ones, and, sure enough, they were the
same gang he and Gerd had run into in the north when
the harpies had shown up. They told about their fright
at the thunder-noises, and about coming back and finding the empty cartridges. This reminded one of the
females of something.

"Big Ones' Friend!" she cried out. "You still have
bright-things? You not lose?"

Little Fuzzy unzipped his shoulder bag and dug out
three fired rifle cartridges and showed them. The female
came over and repossessed them. The Little Fuzzy
found something else in his bag, and cried out.

"I forget! Have shining-stone; find where we work to
make raft in little moving-water."

And he brought out, of all things, a big sunstone. It'd
run about twenty to twenty-five carats. He rubbed it till
it glowed.

"Look! Pretty!"

Grego set Diamond on the floor and came over to
look; so did Diamond. Steefer and Durrante had also
left their chairs.

"Where you get, Little Fuzzy?" Grego asked.

Steefer and Durrante were just swearing. People'd
have to stop swearing around Fuzzies; Little Fuzzy was
beginning to curse like a spaceport labor-boss already.

"Up little moving-water, run, come into lake where
we make camp to make raft."

"You sure you didn't get this here at Yellowsand?"

"I tell you where I get. I not tell you not-so thing."

No, they could depend on that; Fuzzies didn't tell not-so things. Damnit!

"Good God! You know what'll happen if this gets out," Grego said. "Every son of a Khooghra and his brother who can scare up air-vehicles will be swarming in there. We can keep them off Yellowsand, but there's too much country up there. Need an army to police it."

"Why don't *you* operate it?"

Grego's language became as lurid as the forest-fire.

"We need more sunstone-diggings like we need a hole in the head. If our lease is upheld, we'll cut work here to about twenty percent of the present rate. What do you want us to do, flood the market? Get enough sunstones out and they won't be worth the S-450 royalty the Fuzzies are getting."

That was true. They'd had that same trouble with diamonds on Terra, back Pre-Atomic.

"Little Fuzzy," he said, "you found shining-stone, like you tell. Is yours."

"My God, Jack!" Harry Steefer almost howled. "That thing's worth twenty-five grand!"

"That doesn't make a damn's worth of difference. Little Fuzzy found it, it's his. Now listen, Little Fuzzy. You keep, you not lose, not give to anybody. You keep safe, all time. Savvy?"

"Yes, sure. Is pretty. Always want shining-stone."

"You not show to people you not know. Anybody see, maybe be bad Big One, try to take. And anybody ask where you get, you say, Pappy Vic give you, because you find here at Yellowsand."

"But not find here. Find in hard-stone, in little moving-water...."

"I know, I know!" This was what Leslie Coombes and Ernst Mallin always ran into. "Is not-so thing. But you can say."

Little Fuzzy looked puzzled. Then he gave a laugh.

"Sure! Can say not-so thing! Wise One say not-so

thing once. Say he see damnthing; was no damnthing at
all. Tell rest of band, they all think is so.''

"Huh?'' Victor Grego looked at Little Fuzzy, and
then at the Fuzzy with the whistle hung around his neck
and the bandage-turban on his head. "Tell about, Wise
One.''

Wise One shrugged; an Old Terran Frenchman
couldn't have done it better.

"Others want to stay in place, once. I want to go on,
hunt for Big One Place, make friends with Big Ones.
They not want. They afraid, want to stay in same place
all time. So, I tell them big dam'fing come, chase me,
chase Stabber, come eat everybody up. They all frightened. All jump up, make run away up mountain, go
down other side. Then, forget about place they want to
stay, go on to sun's left—to south, like I want.''

One of the females howled like a miniature police-
siren, and not so miniature, either. With his ultrasonic
hearing aid on, it almost shattered Victor's ear.

"You make talk you see hesh-nazza, hesh-nazza come
eat us all up, and no hesh-nazza at all?'' She was dumb-
founded with horrified indignation. "You make us run
away from nice-place, good-to-eat things . . . ?''

"Jeeze-krise sunnabish!'' Wise One shouted at her.
He'd only been around Little Fuzzy a week, and listen
to him. "You think this not nice-place? We stay where
you want, we never see nice-place like this. You make
talk about good-to-eat things; you think we get estee-fee
in place you want to stay? You think we get smokko?
You think we find Big Ones, make friends? You make
bloody-hell talk like big fool!''

"You mean, you told these other Fuzzies you saw a
damnthing and you knew you hadn't at all?'' Grego
demanded. "Well, hallelujah, praise Saint Beelzebub!
You talk to the kids, Jack; I'm going to call Leslie
Coombes right away!''

xxiv.

Hugo Ingermann looked up at the big screen above the empty bench, which showed, like a double-reflecting mirror, a view of the courtroom behind him, filling with spectators. It was jammed, even the balcony above. Well, he'd be playing to a good house, anyhow.

He had nothing to worry about, he told himself. Either way it came out, he'd be safe. If he got his clients acquitted by the faginy and enslavement charges—even a collaboration of Blackstone, Daniel Webster, and Clarence Darrow couldn't do anything with the burglary and larceny charges—that would be that. Of course, he'd be the most execrated man on Zarathustra, with all this publicity about Little Fuzzy and the forest-fire and the rescue, but that wouldn't last. It wouldn't alter the fact that he'd accomplished a courtroom masterpiece, and it would bring clients in droves. *Well, maybe he's a crooked son of a Khooghra, but he's a smart lawyer, you gotta give him that.* And people forgot soon; he knew people. It would bring back a lot of his People's Prosperity Party followers who had defected after he'd been smeared with the gem-vault job. And in a few months, the rush of immigrants would come in, all hoping to get rich on what the CZC had lost, and all sore as hell when they found there was nothing to grab. When they heard that he was the man

who dared buck Ben Rainsford and Victor Grego together, they'd rally to him, and a year after they landed
they'd all be eligible to vote.

If things went sour, he had a line of retreat open. He
congratulated himself on the timing that had accomplished that. He didn't want to have to use it, he wanted
to win here in court, but if anything went wrong . . .

Still, he was tense and jumpy. He wondered if he
oughtn't to take another tranquilizer. No, he'd been
eating those damn things like candy. He started to
straighten the papers on the table in front of him, then
forced his hands to be still. Mustn't let people see him
fidgeting.

A stir in front to the left of the bench; door opened,
jury filing in to take their seats. Now there were twelve
good cretins and true, total IQ around 250. He'd fought
to the death to exclude anybody with brains enough to
pour sand out of a boot with printed directions on the
bottom of the heel. He looked over to the table where
Gus Brannhard was fluffing his whiskers with his left
hand and smiling happily at the ceiling, wondering if
Brannhard had any idea why he'd dragged out the jury
selection for four days.

The other door opened. In came Colonial Marshal
Fane, preceded by his rotund tummy, and then Leo
Thaxter and Conrad and Rose Evins and Phil Novaes,
followed by two uniformed deputies, one of them fon-
dling his pistol-butt hopefully. They were all dressed in
the courtroom outfits he had selected: Thaxter in light
gray—as long as he kept his mouth shut anybody would
take him for a pillar of the community; Conrad Evins in
black, with a dark blue neckcloth; Rose Evins also in
black, relieved by a few touches of pale blue; Phil
Novaes in dark gray, smart but ultraconservative.
Who'd think four respectables like this were a bunch of
fagins and slavers? He got them seated at the table with
him. Thaxter was scowling at the jury.

"Smile, you stupid ape!" he hissed. "Those people

have a 10-mm against the back of your head. Don't make them want to pull the trigger.''

He beamed affectionately at Thaxter. Thaxter's scowl deepened, then he tried, not too successfully, to beam back. He didn't have the face for it.

"You know what's against that back of yours," he whispered.

Yes, and he wished he hadn't put himself in front of it in the first place. Ought to have refused to have anything to do with this case, but, my God . . . !

"Will it start now?" Rose Evins asked.

"Pretty soon. You'll all be called to the stand for arraignment; you'll be under veridication. Now, remember, you only give your names, your addresses, and your civil and racial status—that's Federation citizen, race Terran human. If they ask anything else, refuse to answer. And when they ask you how you plead, you say, 'Not guilty.' Now remember, that's only the way you're pleading. You are not being asked whether you did what you've been charged with or not. When you say, 'Not guilty,' you are making a true statement.''

He went over that again; this had to be hammered in as hard as he could hammer it. He was repeating the caution when there was a stir behind. Looking up at the screen, he saw a procession coming down the aisle. Leslie Coombes and Victor Grego in front—holy God, maybe Grego'd take the stand; just give him a chance to cross-examine!—and Jack Holloway, Gerd and Ruth van Riebeek, George Lunt in uniform, Pancho Ybarra in civvies, Ahmed Khadra, Sandra Glenn—no, Ahmed and Sandra Khadra now—Fitz Morlake, Ernst Mallin . . . the whole damn gang. What a spot to lob a hand-grenade! And six Fuzzies. One wore a light-yellow plastic shoulder bag to match his fur, and the others had blue canvas bags lettered CZC Police, and little police shields on their shoulder-straps. Just as they were getting seated, the crier began chanting, "Rise for the Honorable Court!" and Yves Janiver came in, gray hair and black mustache—must dye the damn thing three times a day, made him look like a villain.

Janiver bowed to the screen and to everybody on Zarathustra who wasn't here in the courtroom, and sat down. The opening formalities were rushed through. Janiver tapped with his gavel.

"A jury having been selected to the mutual satisfaction of the defense and prosecution—you *are* satisfied with the jury, aren't you, gentlemen?—we will proceed with arraignment of the defendants. As this is in Native Cases Court, we will give the visiting team the courtesy of precedence."

The court clerk rose and called Leo Thaxter. Thaxter sat in the witness-chair and had the veridicator helmet let down on his head.

The globe was cerulean blue; it stayed that way, and didn't even flicker on, "Not guilty." Thaxter was an old hand, probably had his first arraignment at age ten on a JD charge. Rose Evins swirled the blue a little; her husband got a few quick stabs of red, trying to avoid some truth he wasn't being asked to tell. The Fuzzies were all sitting on the edge of a table across the room, smoking little cigarette-size cigars and yeek-yeeking among themselves, making ultrasonic comments. Fuzzies were entitled to smoke in court; that was an ancient custom—of all of four months old. Phil Novaes went up to the stand. For him, the globe was a dirty mauve. When he was asked to plead, it blazed like a fire-alarm light. "Not guilty," he said.

"Now, what the hell did you do that for?" Ingermann hissed when Novaes came back.

Everybody in the courtroom was laughing.

"Diamond. Native registration number twenty."

There was an argument among the Fuzzies. The one with the plastic shoulder bag jumped down, ran over to the witness chair, and climbed into it. The human-size helmet was swung aside and a little one swung over and let down. As soon as it touched Diamond's head, he was on his feet.

"Your Honor, I object!"

"And to what, Mr. Ingermann?" the judge asked.

"Your Honor, this Fuzzy is being placed under veridication. It is a known scientific fact that the polyencephalographic veridicator will not detect the difference between true and false statements when made by members of that race." The jury wouldn't know what the hell he was talking about. "A veridicator will not work with a Fuzzy," he added for their benefit.

"You'll have to pardon my abysmal ignorance, Mr. Ingermann, but this alleged scientific fact isn't known to this court."

"It's known to everybody else. Your Honor," he added insultingly. No use trying to avoid antagonizing the court; this court was pre-antagonized already. Maybe he could needle Janiver into saying something exceptionable. "And it is specifically known to the leading specialist in Fuzzy psychology, Dr. Ernst Mallin."

"I seem to see Dr. Mallin here present," Janiver said. "Is that a fact, Doctor Mallin?"

"I must object unless Dr. Mallin veridicates his reply."

Mallin winced. He had a thing about being veridicated in court; he ought to, after what he went through in *People* versus *Kellogg and Holloway*.

"Bloody-go-hell, what you want me make do?" the Fuzzy on the stand demanded.

Everybody ignored that. Janiver said:

"I see no reason why Dr. Mallin should veridicate a simple answer to a simple question; nobody is asking him to give testimony at this time."

"Nobody can give testimony at this time, Your Honor," Coombes said. "The defendants have not all been arraigned."

"What are you trying to do, Ingermann; get a mistrial out of this?" Brannhard said.

"Certainly not!" He was righteously indignant. That was something he hadn't thought of; should have, but too late now. "If the learned court, in what it describes as its abysmal ignorance, seeks enlightenment . . ."

"Doctor Mallin, is it true that, as the learned counsel for the defense states, it is a known fact that Fuzzies cannot be veridicated?"

"Not at all." Mallin was smirking in superiority. "Mr. Ingermann has been listening to mere layman's folklore. As sapient beings, Fuzzies have the same neuro-cerebral system as, say, Terran humans. When they attempt to suppress a true statement and substitute a false one, it is accompanied by the same detectable electromagnetic events."

Whatever that meant to these twelve failed-apprentice morons.

"Dr. Mallin is giving expert testimony, Your Honor. He should be duly qualified as an expert."

"In this court, Mr. Ingermann, Dr. Mallin has long ago been so qualified."

"Your Honor, Mr. Ingermann may get a lot of fun out of this, but I don't," Coombes said. "Let's get these defendants arraigned and get on with the trial."

"It is illegal to place anybody under veridication unless the veridicator has been properly tested."

"This veridicator has been properly tested," Gus Brannhard said. "It red-lighted when your client, Novaes, made the false statement that he was not guilty."

That got a laugh, a real, order-in-the-court laugh; even some of the jury got it. When it subsided, Janiver rapped with his gavel.

"Gentlemen, I seem to recall a law once enacted in some Old Terran jurisdiction, first century Pre-Atomic, to the effect that when two self-propelled ground-vehicles approached an intersection, both should stop and neither start until the other had gone on. That seems to be the situation Mr. Ingermann is trying here to create. He wants to argue that the defendants cannot be arraigned until Dr. Mallin has testified that they can be veridicated, and that Dr. Mallin cannot testify until the defendants have been arraigned. And by that time his clients will have died of old age. Well, I herewith rule that the defendant on the stand, and the other Fuzzy defendants, be arraigned herewith, on the supposition that a veridicator which will work with a human will work with a Fuzzy.''

"Exception!"

"Exception noted. Proceed with the arraignment."

"I warn the court that I will not consider this a precedent for allowing these Fuzzies to testify against my clients."

"That is also to be noted. Proceed, Mr. Clerk."

"What name you?" the clerk asked. "What Big Ones call you?"

"Diamond."

The blue globe over his head became blood-red. *Red!* Oh, holy God, *no!*

"You said they couldn't be veridicated; you said no Fuzzy would red-light—" Evins was jabbering, and Thaxter was saying, "You double-crossing bastard!"

"Shut up, both of you!"

"How I do, Pappy Less'ee?" the Fuzzy, whose name was not Diamond, was asking. "I do like you say?"

"Who is Pappy for you?" the clerk asked.

The Fuzzy thought briefly, said, "Pappy Jack," and got a red light, and then got another when he corrected himself and said, "Pappy Vic."

"You do very good; you good Fuzzy," Leslie Coombes said. "Now, say for is-so what your name."

The Fuzzy said, "Toshi-Sosso. Mean Wise One in Big One talk."

Those damn forest-fire Fuzzies; he was one of them. The veridicator was blue. Rose Evins was saying,

"Well. It looks as though you didn't do it, Mister Ingermann."

The next Fuzzy, called under the name of Allan Pinkerton, made an equally spectacular red-lighting, and then admitted to being called something that meant Stabber. That was good; and just call me Stabbed, Ingermann thought.

"Well, Mr. Ingermann; do I hear any more objections to the veridicated testimony of Fuzzies, or are you willing to be convinced by this demonstration?" Janiver asked. "If so, we will have the real defendants in for arraignment now."

"Well, naturally, Your Honor." What in Nifflheim else could he say? "I must confess myself much deceived. By all means, let the real defendants be arraigned, and after that may I pray the court to recess until 0900 Monday?" That would give him all Saturday, and Sunday . . . "I must confer with my clients and replan the entire defense. . . ."

"What he means, Your Honor, is that now it seems these Fuzzies are going to be allowed to tell the truth, and he doesn't know what to do about it," Brannhard said.

"What the hell are you trying to do, ditch us?" Thaxter wanted to know. "You better not. . . ."

"No, no! Don't worry, Leo; this whole thing's a big fake. I don't know how they did it, but it'd stink on Nifflheim, and by Monday I'll be able to prove it. Just sit tight; everything will be all right if you keep your mouths shut in the meantime."

He looked at his watch. He shouldn't have done that. He shouldn't have given any indication of how vital time was now.

"Well, it's now 1500," Janiver was saying, "and tomorrow's Saturday. There'll be no court, in any case. Yes, Mr. Ingermann; I see no reason for not granting that request."

xxv.

Yves Janiver watched the people in front of him sit down, and wondered how many of them knew. The press hadn't been allowed to get hold of it, but rumor had a million roots and it was probably all over the place. Everybody inside the dividing-rail except the six Fuzzies probably knew, and half the crowd in the spectators' seats. Over to his right, Victor Grego and Leslie Coombes and Jack Holloway and the others were getting the Fuzzies quieted. They all knew. So did Gus Brannhard, with his assistants at the prosecution table; he was almost audibly purring. At the table on the left, Leo Thaxter, Conrad and Rose Evins and Phil Novaes were whispering. Every few seconds, one of them would glance to the rear of the room. Surely they knew. The way rumors circulated in that jail, they probably knew better than anybody else, and maybe up to a quarter of it would be true.

The crier had finished calling the case, naming, one after another, all the people, human and otherwise, who had the Colony of Zarathustra against them. He counted ten seconds, then tapped with the gavel.

"Are we ready?" he asked.

Gus Brannhard rose. "The prosecution is ready, Your Honor."

Leslie Coombes popped up as he sat down. "The defense, for Diamond, Allan Pinkerton, Arsene Lupin, Sherlock Holmes, Irene Adler and Mata Hari is ready."

The names that came before Native Cases Court! Some day, he was sure, he would be trying Mohandas Gandhi and Albert Schweitzer for murder.

The four defendants on his left argued heatedly for a moment. Then Conrad Evins, impelled by his wife, rose and cleared his throat.

"Please the court," he said. "Our attorney seems to have been delayed. If the court will be so good as to wait, I'm sure Mr. Ingermann will be here in a few minutes."

Good Heavens, they didn't know! He wondered what was wrong with the jail-house grapevine. Gus Brannhard was rising again.

"Your Honor, I'm afraid we'll have to wait a trifle more than a few minutes," he said. "I was informed last evening that when the Terra-Baldur-Marduk liner *City of Konkrook* spaced out from Darius at 1430 yesterday, Mr. Hugo Ingermann was aboard as a passenger, with a ticket for Kapstaad Spaceport on Terra. The first port of call en route is New Birmingham, on Volünd. She is now in hyperspace; relative to this space-time continuum, these defendants' counsel is literally nowhere."

There was a sound—the odd, familiar sound that follows a surprise in a courtroom, not unlike an airlock being opened onto lower pressure. More of this crowd than he'd thought hadn't heard about it. There were chuckles, and not all from the Fuzzy defense table.

There was no sound at all from Evins and his co-defendants. Then Evins started. Janiver had seen a man shot once in a duel on Ishtar; his whole body had jerked like that when he had been hit. Rose Evins, who had not risen, merely closed her eyes and relaxed in her chair, her hands loose on the table in front of her. Phil Novaes was gibbering, "I don't believe it! It's a lie! He couldn't do that!" Then Leo Thaxter was on his feet, bellowing obscenities.

"You mean we don't have any lawyer?" Evins was demanding.

"Is this absolutely certain, Mr. Brannhard?" the judge asked, for the record.

Brannhard nodded gravely, the gravity a trifle forced.

"Absolutely, Your Honor. I had it from Mr. Grego here, who had it from Terra-Baldur-Marduk on Darius. I saw a photoprint of the passenger list with Mr. Ingermann's name, special luxury-cabin accommodations."

"Yes, that's how the son of a bitch would be traveling," Thaxter shouted. "On our money. You know what he took with him? Two hundred and fifty thousand sols in sunstones!"

There was another whoosh of surprise from in front. It even extended to the Fuzzy defense table. Grego snapped his fingers and said audibly, "By God, that's it! That's where they went!" The judge graveled briskly and called for order; the crier repeated the call, and the uproar died away.

"You will have to repeat that statement under veridication, Mr. Thaxter," he said.

"Don't worry, I will," Thaxter told him. "What we'll tell about that crook . . ."

"What we want to know," Evins said, "is what about us? We have a legal right to a lawyer. . . ."

"You had a lawyer. You should have chosen a better one. Now sit down, you people, and be quiet. The court is quite aware of your legal rights, and will appoint a counsel for you."

Who the devil would that be? This crowd had no money to hire a lawyer; the Colony would have to pay the fee. It would have to be a good one, with a solid reputation. Janiver was, himself, convinced of the guilt of all four of them; that meant he'd have to lean over backward to give them a scrupulously fair trial before sentencing them to be shot.

"Your Honor." Leslie Coombes was on his feet. "I move for dismissal of the charges against my clients." He named them. "They are here charged on complaints brought by Hugo Ingermann, who has since absconded from the planet, merely as a maneuver to discredit the charges against his own clients."

"Motion granted; these six Fuzzies should not have been charged in the first place." He said that over, in the proper phraseology, and discharged the six Fuzzies from the custody of the court.

"Since these remaining defendants are entitled to the legal aid and advice of which the defection of their attorney has deprived them, I will continue this case on Monday of next week, by which time the court will have appointed a new counsel for them, and he will have had opportunity to familiarize himself with the case and consult with them. Marshal Fane, will you return the defendants to the jail? We will now take up the next ready case on the docket."

The Government was a representative popular democracy—the Federation Constitution said it had to be —and the Charterless Zarathustra Company was a dictatorship. One difference is that when a dictator wants privacy, he gets it. So, though they would have dinner at Government House, they were having koktel-drinko in Grego's office at Company House. The Fuzzies were all at the Fuzzy Club, entertaining Wise One and his band, who were completely flabbergasted about everything, but deliriously happy.

Grego and Coombes were drinking cocktails. Gus, of course, had a water tumbler full of whiskey, and a bottle within reach to take care of evaporation-loss. Ben Rainsford had a highball, very weak. Jack had a highball, rather less so. He set it down to light his pipe, and didn't pick it up again. He was going to make this one last as long as he could.

"Well, it's a new high in disposal costs," Coombes was saying. "Two hundred and fifty thousand sols to get rid of Hugo Ingermann seems just a bit exorbitant."

"It's worth it," Grego told him. "He'd have cost us a couple of million if he'd stayed on this planet. It'll be up to you to cut the cost as much as you can."

"Well, I can get judgments against everything he left, but that isn't much. One thing, we have all that property in North Mallorysport. Now we don't need to be afraid that somebody like Pan-Federation or Terra-Odin will get hold of it and put in a spaceport to compete with Terra-Baldur-Marduk on Darius."

"What I want to know," Ben Rainsford began, frowning into his drink, "is how Ingermann got hold of those sunstones. I don't understand how they even got out of Company House."

"Oh, that's easy," Gus Brannhard said. "We got all that out of Evins and Thaxter this afternoon. The Fuzzies didn't take them out of the gem-vault at all. Evins had taken them out in his pockets a couple of days before. He stashed them in a locker at the Mallorysport-Darius space terminal and mailed the key to a poste-restante code-number. He memorized the number and gave it to Ingermann after he was arrested. Ingermann lifted the stones for his fee. What that did, it made Ingermann liable to accessory-after-the-fact and receiving-stolen-goods charges. Evins and his wife and Thaxter thought they could control Ingermann that way. Well, you see how it worked."

"Well, won't they catch up with Ingermann?"

"Huh-uh. We'll send out a warrant for him, but you know how slow interstellar communication is. What he'll do, as soon as he lands on Terra he'll take another ship out for somewhere else. There only are about twenty spaceships leaving Terra every day, for all over the galaxy. He'll get to some planet like Xipototec or Fenris or Ithavoll Lugaluru and dig in there, and nobody'll ever find him. Who wants to find him? I don't.''

"Well, what's going to be done about Thaxter and the Evinses and Novaes? That's what I want to know," Rainsford said. "They're not going to walk away from this, are they?''

"Oh, no," Gus Brannhard assured him. "Janiver appointed Douglas Toyoshi to defend them; Doug and Janiver and I got together in Janiver's chambers and made a deal. They'll plead guilty to the sunstone charges, and will immediately be sentenced, ten-to-twenty years. After that, they will be put on trial on the faginy and enslavement charges. There's no question about their being convicted.''

"Faginy too?" Coombes asked.

"Faginy too. Toyoshi will accept Pendarvis's minor-child ruling. Not that that will matter in principle; the whole body of the Pendarvis Decisions, minor-child status and all, is going into the Colonial Constitution. Well, when they are convicted of enslavement and faginy, they will be sentenced to be shot, separately on each charge, two sentences to a customer. Execution will be deferred until they have completed their prison sentences, and the death sentences will then be subject to review by the court.''

Coombes laughed. "They won't be likely to bother the parole board in the meantime," he commented.

"No. And I doubt, after twenty years, if any court would order them shot. They're getting just about what they paid Ingermann to get them.''

No; there was a big difference. They'd be convicted and sentenced, and that was what Jack wanted: to get it established that the law protected Fuzzies the same as other people. He said so, and finished his drink, wondering if he oughtn't to have another. Grego had said something about Ingermann, and Rainsford laughed.

"Wise One and his gang are heroes all over again, for running him off Zarathustra." He laughed again. "Chased out by a gang of Fuzzies!"

"What's going to happen to them? They can't be career heroes the rest of their lives."

"They won't have to be," Coombes said. "I have adopted the whole eight of them."

"What?"

The Company lawyer nodded. "That's right. Got the adoptions fixed up Saturday. I am now Pappy Less'ee, with papers to prove it." He finished his cocktail. "You know, I never realized till I brought that gang in last Monday what I was missing." He looked around, at Pappy Vic and Pappy Jack and Pappy Ben and Pappy Gus. "You all know what I mean."

"But you're going to Terra after the general election; you'll be gone for a couple of years. Who'll take care of them while you're gone?"

"I will. I am taking my family with me," Coombes said.

The idea of taking Fuzzies off Zarathustra hadn't occurred to Jack Holloway, and he was automatically against it.

"It'll be all right, Jack. Juan Jimenez's people tell me that a Fuzzy will be perfectly able to adapt to Terran conditions; won't even need to adapt. They'll be as healthy there as they are here."

That much was right. Conditions were practically identical on both planets.

"And they'll be happy, Jack," Coombes was saying. "They just want to be with Pappy Less'ee. You know, I never had anybody love me the way those Fuzzies do. And everybody on Terra will be crazy about them."

That was it. That was what Fuzzies wanted, more than chopper-diggers and shoulder bags, more than rifles and things to play with and learning about the Big Ones' talk-marks, more even than Extee Three: Affection. It had been the need for that, he knew now, that had brought Little Fuzzy to him out of the woods, and the others after him. More than anything he could give, it was Little Fuzzy's promise that all Fuzzies would have Big Ones of their own to love them and take care of them and be good to them that appealed to the Fuzzies at Hoksu-Mitto. They needed affection as they needed air and water, just as all children did.

That was what they were—permanent children. The race would mature, sometime in the far future. But meanwhile, these dear, happy, loving little golden-furred children would never grow up. He picked up his glass and finished it, then sat holding it, looking at the ice in it, and felt a great happiness relaxing him. He hadn't anything to worry about. The Fuzzies wouldn't ever turn into anything else. They'd just stay Fuzzies: active, intelligent children, who loved to hunt and romp and make things and find things out, but children who would always have to be watched over and taken care of and loved. He must have realized that, subconsciously, from the beginning when he'd started Little Fuzzy to calling him Pappy Jack.

And, gosh! Eight Fuzzies going for a big-big trip with Pappy Less'ee. New things to see, and Pappy Less'ee to show them everything and tell them about it. And after a few years, they'd all come back . . . and all the wonderful things they'd have to tell.

He let Grego take his glass and mix him another high-ball, then picked it up and relighted the pipe that had gone out.

Damned if he didn't wish sometimes that *he* was a Fuzzy!

THE WORLDS OF H. BEAM PIPER